A Brush with Napoleon

A BRUSH WITH NAPOLEON

An Encounter with
Jacques-Louis David

LABAN CARRICK HILL

WATSON-GUPTILL PUBLICATIONS
NEW YORK

First published in 2007 by Watson-Guptill Publications,
a division of VNU Business Media, Inc.
770 Broadway, New York, NY 10003
www.watsonguptill.com

ISBN-13: 978-0-8230-0417-1
ISBN-10: 0-8230-0417-1

Printed in the U.S.A.
First printing, 2007
1 2 3 4 5 6 7 8 9 / 14 13 12 11 10 09 08 07

For Susan Cohen, Jackie Ching,
and my daughters, Natalie and Ella.

Contents

Preface

"Beauty is truth, truth beauty," — that is all
Ye know on earth, and all ye need to know.

These last lines in "Ode on a Grecian Urn" by the Romantic poet John Keats put forth a proposition. Beauty — and by extension art — can embody the great and noble truths that transcend all ages. As Keats gazed upon an ancient Greek urn decorated with figures, he found himself meditating on the meaning of such beauty. At the end of the poem when the urn finally speaks and says "Beauty is truth, truth beauty," Keats seems to be saying that indeed beauty does embody truth.

And yet those quotation marks throw into doubt Keats's own belief in this truism. An object, not the poet, says these lines, the poet himself is not so sure and takes pains to alert the reader of this fact. The question raised in *A Brush with Napoleon* is just this, Can art embody absolute truth?

Seventeen-year-old Jean finds himself a student of a great master painter who has staked his reputation on art being the embodiment of perfection and moral truths. In the late eighteenth century, the painter

Jacques-Louis David was one of the originators of a school of painting called Neoclassicism. Neoclassicism was a response to the playful style of Rococo art, which in the face of such social and political turmoil of the times (the French Revolution) seemed trivial and excessive. David and his Neoclassicist contemporaries valued the formal elements of line and form over color. They considered the proper subjects for art to be moralizing themes of grand historical significance.

For David, this initially meant painting scenes from ancient Greek and Roman history. These scenes spoke to the contemporary turmoil of the corruption of the king's government, the revolution and the hopes and dreams for what the new era would bring. The real breakthrough artistically for David was his *The Oath of Horatii*. Commissioned by the Administrator of Royal Residences in 1784 and exhibited at the 1785 Salon, this masterpiece was taken from Titus-Livy. It depicted the period of the wars between Rome and Alba, in 669 B.C.E. The drama behind the image is the decision that the two cities must settle their disagreement by an unusual form of combat to be fought by two groups of three champions each. The two groups are the three Horatii brothers and the three Curiatii brothers. The drama lay in the fact that one of the sisters of the Curiatii, Sabina, is married to one of the Horatii, while one of the sisters of the Horatii, Camilla, is betrothed to one of the Curiatii. Despite the ties between the two families, the Horatii's father exhorts his sons to fight the Curiatii and they obey, despite the lamentations of the women.

In this masterpiece, the clothing and architecture are based on actual historical examples from Roman antiquity. The monumental figures are arranged in rigid poses across a shallow space in imitation of sculptural decorations called friezes found in classical buildings. In the stage-like setting of the painting, the harsh lighting and cool colors emphasize the crisp, hard outlines that define the forms in the composition. The surface of the painting is smooth and highly finished, emphasizing the firmly modeled forms. The brushwork is almost invisible to suggest a visual perfection unlike anything seen before. All of this transforms the composition into a solemn act that binds the wills of different individuals into a single, creative gesture. As a result, David's painting succeeds in ennobling these passions and transforming the virtues that the participants exhibit into something sublime.

When *A Brush with Napoleon* begins, David has long established himself as *the* premier painter in France with his historical paintings. Now, however, he has been caught up in the frenzy and excitement of the new Republic and has decided to apply his artistic vision to contemporary events. In the painting *Napoleon Crossing the Alps at the Saint Bernard Pass*, David attempts to infuse a contemporary event with the same nobility as his ancient scenes. Could he capture a contemporary figure—Napoleon—and freeze him in time while he was still in the midst of creating history? How much realism can intrude on a painting that had to inspire a nation and spur an army on to seemingly endless warfare? Could art, and the artifice of re-creating a contemporary scene, embody the essential truths of the new republic, truths that were still in the process of being articulated? These are the questions this book—and David's art—struggle with.

"Truth is not half so important as what people think to be true."
—Napoleon

CHAPTER 1

Battle in the Alps

*B*oom!

Bone-shattering explosions rocked his body. Napoleon's cannons fired in steady succession, one after another like a metronome without interruption.

Boom!

His ribcage felt as if it would detonate. As part of Napoleon's army, he was running toward these explosions.

Boom!

Dirt clods rained around him from above. Stones slammed the ground. "The sky *is* falling," he laughed, remembering the old fairytale his mother used to tell him when he was young. "I must be insane."

Boom!

"Humpfff!" He couldn't breathe. It was like a huge boot had stomped hard on his chest. All the air was gone. None was coming in.

Boom! Boom! Boom!

Like a rag doll, he was suddenly flipped on his back. "Come on, Jean!" shouted the soldier with sergeant stripes as he lifted Jean up by the belt.

Suddenly, the air rushed back into his lungs. "Alain," Jean gasped. He coughed.

Alain's big, meaty hand gripped seventeen-year-old private Jean Martin by the collar and yanked him to his feet. "Your father would kill me if I let you die in your first battle." Alain raised his rifle and fired. "Hunch over when you run." He bent slightly at the waist and ran forward. "That way the force of the explosions don't hit you full on."

Jean crouched and followed. "Well, Papa's dead, so he won't know the difference," he answered with a false sense of bravado. In fact, like any sane person, Jean was terrified.

Napoleon's cannons echoed across the valley with the striking regularity of a giant thundering drum.

The assault began long before the sun crawled above the mountains as the Armée de Réserve flowed out of the St. Bernard mountain pass. Overhead, the ridges seemed like shadows over shadows. Though the rain had stopped, there still was no moon and the stars seemed even more distant behind the dissipating clouds.

The two soldiers dove head first into a crater made by an exploded shell. "I promised your father I'd treat you like my own son." Alain grimaced as he rolled onto his back to reload his musket. "And I'll be damned if I'll let you die in the Alps after I'd saved your scrawny little ass in Egypt."

"Saved my life?" Jean laughed.

"I got you assigned to the rear with Napoleon's artists, who were brought along to record our triumphs," said Alain with sarcasm: The Egyptian campaign was an unmitigated disaster.

"You would still have had me back with the women if you'd had your way." The memories of Egypt quickly flashed in his mind. Though the campaign might have been nearly ruinous for Napoleon, it had been a triumph for Jean. He had discovered his life's passion, and it wasn't war.

"Damn right." Alain fixed his bayonet on the end of his musket.

"Those Austrian bastards are asleep," shouted another soldier who fell into the crater.

As wave after wave of Napoleon's advance guard attacked the walled village, the garrison in Aosta yielded with surprising ease. A few Austrian soldiers offered resistance, firing their muskets without aiming at the advancing French soldiers before hastily retreating.

The sound of intermittent rifle fire echoed through the dark valley. In such chaos it was unclear who was shooting at whom or exactly where the enemy was. Jean witnessed a soldier shot down by one of his own. Still, the brigade advanced. The torches along the village walls offered direction, and the sight of the retreating Austrians goaded Jean and his fellow soldiers.

"Don't stop now," shouted Alain. "We've got them on the run, and this'll be over fast." He kicked a conscript in his rear end to urge him forward.

"I'm glad we caught…" A musket ball grazed Jean's blue wool sleeve, and he urinated in his pants. For all his tough talk of being on the Egyptian campaign, Alain was right, Jean had never actually seen combat. Whenever the army had encountered resistance from Arabs, he had been safely at the rear of the column, in the comfort of the artists who were there to paint, not fight.

Jean froze, staring at the hole in his jacket. The ball had missed his arm completely, but the hole proved just how close he had come to injury. He glanced around and saw the others pressing forward despite the return fire. Self-consciously he tried to laugh it off, like it was something he was used to, but the chill of his cooling urine belied such false courage. Despite the terror, or perhaps because of it, he ran forward with even more abandon, hurling himself at the enemy.

On the run, he pulled his long bayonet and hurriedly mounted it onto his musket. He had fired and did not want to stop and reload, making himself a stationary target. The field that they were crossing was small and with no clear barriers to hide behind. Shoulder to shoulder, his brigade attacked, a wall of blue uniforms moving quickly at the terrified Austrians.

"We've broken their lines," came a shout out of the chaos. A cheer followed.

As the soldiers surged forward, Jean almost gagged from the strange smell of burnt gunpowder and soldiers soiling themselves. At the same time, he was aware of his breath rushing in and out. Every part of his being felt on edge. He spotted the muzzle of a sniper's rifle up in a bell tower. The musket appeared to be pointed right at Alain. In an instant, Jean dove toward Alain and pulled him to the ground. The shot fired wide, hitting the ground within inches of them.

Without stopping even to thank his friend, Alain pulled Jean to his feet and pushed him forward. "Let's move! They're ours!"

This is war. This is war, Jean kept repeating in his mind to the metronome of his beating heart. *Don't stop. Don't stop...or you're dead.*

Once the Austrian soldiers regrouped behind the walls, they seemed to muster courage and returned fire rapidly. Their four- and eight-pound cannons discharged only once before Napoleon's advance guard poured over the walls. Panicking, the Austrians dropped their muskets and retreated without order. If it had not been in the middle of a battle, their retreat would have been comical, the way they abandoned their positions tripping over each other.

"Don't let them get away!" shouted the captain. "We can't allow them to warn the army at Marengo."

Jean watched Alain trip an Austrian and then smash the butt of his musket into the soldier's head. As Alain subdued another soldier, Jean ran ahead and swung his musket like a club, almost taking off the head of another Austrian. Without looking back, he went after another. The entire brigade worked to capture the enemy with an extraordinary glee as they released their pent-up fear. Some loaded their muskets and took target practice on the terrified enemy. By then, Jean's brigade seemed more at play than at battle.

"Watch this!" shouted one French soldier. He fired his musket and an Austrian soldier went down.

"Let me try that!" Another soldier fired but missed his target.

Laughter erupted. The cruel games of the victor had begun.

"Bring the prisoners to the square," shouted an officer who led half a dozen captured Austrian infantrymen. Unprovoked, a French soldier clubbed the head of an Austrian. Blood cascaded down the prisoner's face as his comrades picked him up. The officer in charge ignored his soldier's violence, acting as if such brutality was not only expected, but justified. The French brigade had won, and so it was their right to take vengeance.

The entire skirmish lasted less than an hour, but the chaos and adrenaline the fight unleashed did not diminish immediately.

Two soldiers kicked in the door of a butcher and stole—or what they called "liberated"—whatever they could. Another group of soldiers emerged from the church with their arms full of reliquaries. No one seemed in command as the town was being looted. The contrast between the current chaos and the controlled and disciplined attack was extraordinary. The men had been unprepared for so little resistance. Their aggression now was unleashed on the citizens of Aosta.

As some of the men gathered in the village square, Sergeant Alain Marquand found Jean. "You have any money?" He leaned on his musket breathing heavily. Rivulets of sweat ran down his face despite it being cold enough to see his breath.

Jean reached into his jacket. "A sous." He handed it over. Then he examined the holes in his sleeve. The fabric was burned around the edges of the entry and exit holes. He stuck his finger through them.

"You've been baptized," laughed Alain. "It's better than any priest could do. If a bullet misses you like that in your first battle, you'll never need worry about being hit. It's a sign from God." The sergeant grabbed Jean by the hole in his sleeve. "This way, my hero!" He pulled Jean down a side street and stopped at a hut with a café sign hanging above the door. The windows were shuttered.

"They're closed at this time of morning," Jean said.

"No, they're not." The sergeant banged his fist on the door. "No one sleeps through all this." He smashed his fist against the door again. "I'll kick the door down!" he shouted roughly.

A man in nightclothes holding a candle swung open the door. He looked terrified. "I have nothing of value."

"What? Were you hiding in the cellar?" Alain pushed the man aside and entered.

The proprietor followed silently.

"Two cognacs!" commanded Alain as he held up two bloodstained fingers.

Jean followed. He was still excited by the battle and didn't quite know what to do with himself or what to make of Alain. He was just happy that Alain had included him.

"Please, have a seat." The owner waved a hand toward a table with two chairs by the door.

"Drink!" commanded the sergeant. He smacked three coins onto the table.

The man nodded. Without a word he poured two large mugs and set them on the table. He hesitated at the table, looking at the money.

Alain waved. "It's yours."

The proprietor still did not take the money. "It's my pleasure."

"Go on! I pay for my drink."

The man scooped the change away and disappeared into a back room.

The sergeant leaned forward conspiratorially. "You know I loved your father."

"Yes, sergeant."

"You are family now."

"So you said," said Jean.

"Good." He drank. "Your papa taught me how to read and write. I will never forget that."

Jean took a small sip. He was exhausted and thought he might pass out if he drank much. He could barely remember his parents. When he was a baby his mother had secured a job as a laundress for the army so the family was able to stay together. Every few days, his father would suddenly appear at his side as he played with the other soldiers' children. His father would pull out his chess set and teach him the game, and they would play until he had to return to his unit a few hours later. Always, the last game, he would let Jean win. For a long time Jean believed he could truly beat his father, but as he grew older he could see his father make obvious mistakes to ensure that the boy won.

Jean's mother died when he was twelve. By then, Jean had learned to wring the necks of chickens in the army's mess. He hated the job, but for a boy as small as he was, the only other place in the army was as part of the drumming corps. Jean's father did not want him so close to danger, so the kitchen was the only choice. Three years later, his father died from dysentery, a horrible and painful death that stretched out over several weeks. Jean got himself reassigned to the hospital and tended to his father during his final days. When his father had finally succumbed, Alain had shown up at the burial and taken Jean to his commander. He was fifteen, the army was preparing for the Egyptian

campaign, and Alain's captain made arrangements for Jean to billet with
the artists. When the army returned from Egypt in tatters, Jean trans-
ferred to Alain's brigade.

"I will watch out for you as if you were my son." Alain turned
toward the back of the café. "A carafe of water!"

The café owner returned with the carafe and a second mug for
Alain.

Alain picked up the water and promptly poured it on Jean's lap.

Jean leapt back in surprise, turning his chair over.

"There. Your pants are now clean." Alain set the carafe back on the
table. "Everyone pisses in their pants. I worry about the ones who
don't. They don't know fear, and that's really dangerous." He patted
Jean on the back. "But I know you're a real soldier because you didn't
crap in them, too."

Jean smiled as he picked up his chair. He had passed some sort of
test in Alain's eyes, and he was grateful. For a while, the two sat silently
staring into their drinks. Alain periodically taking large gulps, while
Jean drank sparingly, only enough to keep his body warm as his cold,
wet pants dried on him.

"And you saved my life," said Alain raising his mug. "For that I am
grateful. And my wife is grateful. And my daughter is grateful. And my
son is grateful. We thank you!" He drained his mug.

The café door banged open, and a soldier looked in. "Let's move it!
On to Marengo!"

CHAPTER 2

Collapse at Marengo

"Damn," Alain said under his breath.

On one side, Jean crouched reloading his musket. On the other, the new recruit from Brittany was no longer a new recruit. The front half of his skull was gone.

As easy as the assault on Aosta was, Marengo was brutal. Jean and Alain found themselves pinned down behind a low stone wall. Enemy cannon fire sailed overhead, and the cries of the wounded intertwined with the sounds of battle.

Alain pulled a biscuit out of his pocket, broke it, and handed one half to Jean. "Eat! Eat!" he growled. "We won't have time later." Both gnawed on their flat piece of biscuit hard as stone, and waited. Neither one wanted to move from the safety of the wall, but both knew that eventually they would have to. Sitting still was more dangerous than moving on a battlefield of shifting advantage. After a few minutes, Alain placed his blue shako, the tall military hat that the soldiers of the 57th Ligne wore, on the end of his musket. The 57th were nicknamed "the Terrible" for their fierce fighting.

"This is the oldest trick, but it's the only way to find out if you've been spotted without getting your head blown off." Alain winked at Jean.

A moment later, Alain raised the shako above the lip of the wall. He bobbed it up and down as if someone were crawling and had not realized his head was above the wall. After what seemed like several minutes, but in reality was a few seconds, he looked his shako over. A bullet had not pierced the hat. Alain took it as a good sign. "Let's go." He leaped over the wall, raised his musket, and fired. He motioned for Jean to follow as he reloaded.

Jean crawled over the wall and sprawled on the ground. When Alain readied his musket, they charged the Austrian defenses.

"Arrrrggghhhh!" Others of the unit joined them, and the ragged line began to re-form and press forward.

Before them lay the dead and wounded from earlier assaults by both armies. The ground was slippery from all the blood and gore. Jean struggled to keep his footing and press forward. This time he held his bladder in check, and even the mangled dead did not turn his stomach. His eyes only flicked across those who had fallen, as he focused on the enemy defenses. Some were his friends, some his enemies, but all now gone.

In front of him, Alain moved like a deer springing across a meadow. His ease and sure-footed movement in the face of musket and cannon fire shocked him. He could detect a kind of crazed fury in his friend's face, which scared him as much as the enemy. He would do anything not to disappoint Alain. Out of this emotion his courage brimmed almost to recklessness. As he quickly found his footing, he dashed among musket balls searing the choking, smoke-filled air.

Tripping, his hand shot out to catch himself, and he landed on the blank, dead face of their captain. The cold body of the captain lay with a hole in his chest the size of Jean's fist.

"No!" Jean recoiled and almost turned to run back toward his own lines, but he gritted his teeth and pressed on behind Alain. "Nothing will stop me," he growled.

The cries of agony rose like a chorus to the percussive cannon fire. High shrieks of musket fire sliced the air.

"Jean! Please!" A friend he had made during the march over the Alps lay with his left arm missing. Blood poured in spurts from the wound. "Help me," he gasped as the life flowed out of him.

Jean saw him die out of the corner of his eye, but he willed himself not to stop. Jean wanted to help his comrade. *I know how*, he reminded himself in the instant that he dashed past. While he had nursed his dying father, he had learned to dress wounds and attend to the sick in the hospital. *But this is war. Can't stop. This is war. Can't stop*, he thought to the rhythm of his own breathing.

"Jean!" Alain called as he fired and reloaded his musket.

The boy glanced ahead.

"Forget the wounded!"

"I wasn't…" Jean tried to explain that he wasn't going to help them, but he stopped when he realized that any argument or discussion was too absurd to even begin.

A column of Austrian infantrymen stood fifty yards away with their muskets raised. They fired. Miraculously, none hit Jean or Alain.

The joy of his sheer luck allowed Jean to abandon all sense of fear and reserve. He heard himself shout, "Kill them!" as he surged forward.

From up on the ridge, cannon fire began to rain down on them. As the cannonballs hit the ground, they exploded with shrapnel, which struck the soldiers around him. The entire battlefield seemed to slow down. Jean's senses felt so keen that he thought he might even be able to see a musket ball coming straight at him and still have time to dodge it. He had an uncanny sense of control, right at the moment when he was losing it. His body was falling. As Jean fought against the inevitable pull of gravity, he raised his musket and tried to fire, but for some reason the gun would not respond. Instead, he watched it slip from his hands. The musket fell, and despite reaching out for it, the distance between Jean and the gun seemed to stretch farther and farther until it seemed as if he and the weapon were at opposite ends of the battlefield.

In training, he had been told over and over again never to let his Charleville, the name of the musket's manufacturer and its nickname among the troops, become muddy or fouled in any way. Jean felt a sudden sense of desperation as the musket fell from his grasp. The battle around him was forgotten, and only his concern for the Charleville existed. He tried to speak to the musket, to call it back into his hands the way he might command a dog.

Panic. The word *panic* suddenly sprung into his head, but he wasn't certain what the word meant anymore.

"Jean!" He could hear Alain shouting, but he couldn't make out the words. Alain's voice seemed to echo down a long tunnel.

Jean took a step, but his legs did not respond. He simply continued to fall and fall and fall. Something, he was not sure what, was pulling on him. Someone had grabbed hold of him and was pulling him down. He wanted to brush the hands away, but his arms would not follow his commands. With a sudden thud, his body stopped moving. In his mind he knew this meant he had hit the ground, but he could not feel the ground. He could not feel anything. The sounds of battle, the agony of the dying, even the words of Alain were now silent.

On the edge of his vision he could see the Austrians advancing. They had fixed their bayonets to the ends of their muskets. In the morning sunlight the finely honed blades gleamed with menace and he could do nothing about it. Helpless, he watched them bayonet enemy soldiers—his comrades. Once again, his mind willed his hands to find his Charleville, but still they would not follow his orders. Slowly, he moved his head and saw why. His right arm lay useless. The cloth of his uniform sleeve had been stripped, and his skin had been scraped clean. A raw, bloody pulp of muscle and bone was horribly exposed. He saw his own blood coursing from his body. Jean thought of his friend whose blood he watched pump out of him until he was dead.

Only then did the pain explode so incredibly that Jean nearly passed out.

Without warning, he was lifted up off the ground. He could not turn to see who was carrying him, but he knew it must be Alain.

After what could have been a minute or an hour or a year later, there was an explosion. Thrown out of Alain's arms, Jean became weightless, unmoored from the battlefield, from the earth. In a surprising moment of clarity, he wondered, *Is this death?* but before he could answer, the world stopped. Nothing. Not even an awareness of nothing. Simply nothing.

CHAPTER 3

A Field Hospital

Hot! Damn! Hot! The sand burns like white coals through my boots. A thick coat of mud paints my tongue like black tar. It has been three days since my last drop of water. Three days! Three days for the entire army!

Waking in a field hospital. The smell of death and dying. The rasp of saws grinding through bone. The rot of flesh. The flies.

Jean blinks. *This is not the desert. This is not Egypt,* he realizes. He's been hallucinating. *Where am I?*

He lay tied to a cot. His last memory was of weightlessness, a kind of floating above and away from the battlefield, but that was all intertwined with memories of Egypt. As his head cleared a little, he became aware that Egypt and the battlefield are not the same. "Egypt was two years ago," he mumbled. "This is…this is…." For the life of him he couldn't remember, but the strain to do so made him pass out once more.

We're going to live. We're going to live. The sweet flesh of watermelon is like an elixir of life. So juicy. I could eat these huge melons for the rest of my life. Every day. The cool feel of the sticky juice dribbling down my chin. So wonderful. Now I won't die in the desert. We've made it to the Nile and found acres of watermelon patches. Could this be the manna the Bible speaks of?

Jean jolted awake. He tried to sit up but couldn't. Someone had tied him down. He was unable to move his arms or legs. As he struggled to find the strength to pull himself free, he soiled himself. He could do nothing about it. Not that he cared. He was in no condition to care about dignity or appearance. He simply wanted to know what hell he was in now. Moving his head caused excruciating pain.

Puking. I'm going to puke my stomach through my throat. Everywhere around me men are puking. The melons have made us sick. We can't hold them down. I am going to die!

Minutes, hours, or perhaps days later, he had no way of knowing, he simply woke again. The time he spent unconscious was lost, as if it never existed.

All he could do was stare at the roof of the tent and wait. He wanted to be grateful that he was still alive, but the cries of pain all around him made him think that he might be wrong. That instead he was dead in his own private hell.

"Manal, my love."

"Don't be a fool." She is Egyptian, but she is also a Christian.

I reach out and place my hand on her soft breast.

Delirious, he considered whether they had tied him down so that he would not drift away. Perhaps his body's weight had not fully returned. If this was so, he was also grateful for whoever had done it.

Before he moved beyond these thoughts, he passed out.

"Thank you, Baron."

"If you are to carry my inks and pens, then you must learn to draw."

"I want to."

"Napoleon brought me to record his triumphs in my etchings. You will do the same."

Awake again, later. Much later. How long? It didn't occur to Jean to wonder. This time he was aware that he was not alone. He turned his head. The pain was searing, but out of the corner of his eye he saw what seemed to be a sea of wounded men on cots. He could not sit up to see how far the cots went. He stared at the tent fabric above him and listened to the unrelenting sounds of agony surrounding him.

"Kill me! Kill me! Kiiillllllll...."

"Water! Water!"

"Help me! Somebody please help me!"

Jean wondered where his voice had gone but fell asleep before an answer came to him.

The feet of a camel are so hard to capture on paper. The way the two toes splay outward under the weight. The curve of each toe and how the toenail emerges mysteriously from the matted fur are nearly impossible to capture with a pencil. I just want to reach out, hold a foot in my hand, feel the bone under the soft flesh, and test how the weight changed its shape. Then maybe I could make a drawing that would please Baron Denon.

It was dark now. *What time was it? What day?* Jean remembered drinking with Alain in that café in Aosta, but as he relived stepping out the door his memory vanished. It was if he had stepped off an abyss. Time beyond that moment was unreachable, untouchable. His past beyond that point had been wiped away like a lesson on a chalkboard.

Who was that? A woman leaned over him and wiped his brow.

"Manal," he whispered through his dry lips and smiled. He slipped his hand from his binding. "Manal," he croaked again. His hand reached up, and he placed it on her breast.

"What!" The young nurse jumped back. "You are delirious, but that doesn't mean you can take advantage of me." She tied his wrist down, this time more securely.

"Manal, kiss me."

Her smile swam in and out of his consciousness like a ripple across a pond.

"Manal," he repeated.

And then came the pain.

The sound of footsteps coming closer. A doctor wearing a blood-soaked apron wended his way through the rows of cots. As he came upon Jean, he stopped and placed a cool hand on his forehead. "He has a fever," the doctor said to the young nurse who had been following him. "Put him to sleep and bleed him."

The nurse nodded grimly. "Yes, father."

Jean heard her response and wondered if he was back in the monastery in the St. Bernard Pass. The nurse's long brown hair was tied up around her head like a halo.

"An angel," he whispered. "An angel," he repeated, and forever he believed she would remain so.

The pretty nurse crossed the tent to a medicine cabinet. She unlocked a small case on a shelf and extracted a bottle filled with a yellowish liquid, laudanum. The powerful drug was a tincture of opium suspended in alcohol. She uncorked the bottle and poured a measured amount into a cup. Adding water, she stirred the mixture. On another shelf she took down a jar filled with writhing leeches. The brown-and-gray fingerlike creatures shimmered in wetness as she selected a two-inch leech and placed it on a cloth.

She returned to Jean's bedside, knelt beside the cot and patiently emptied the laudanum into his mouth. Jean choked on the liquid. Within minutes, he was asleep again. The nurse then laid his left arm flat and placed the leech on a vein on the inside of his arm. Quietly and with almost no discernable movement, the leech bit through the skin and drank of the young man's blood.

CHAPTER 4

Awake Among the Dying

"Alain!" shouted Jean, waking himself up from a dream. "I have to help Alain." He tore at his bindings with such fury he no longer felt his pain. "I can't leave him!"

The large hospital tent throbbed like a giant organism of pain and rotting flesh. Without rest, doctors, nurses, and attendants moved among the wounded as if performing rituals that had no hope of succeeding.

Jean freed his arms and ripped at the strips of fabric that tied his legs to the cot.

"Alain!"

He untied his legs and swung them off the cot. Blood quickly soaked through the bandages wrapped around his right leg and his arm, but he was oblivious to it. His only concern was finding his friend, his surrogate father. In his stupor, Jean was desperately afraid he had lost him and that somehow it was his fault. Memories of his father dying in agony and his mother suddenly falling ill and dying rushed into his consciousness. The awful emptiness and powerlessness and panic of that experience reemerged in his delusional state.

"Not this time!" he shouted as hands pressed his shoulders. "I won't allow it. I won't lose Alain, too." Jean slashed at the bindings that held him safely to the cot. He ripped at the bandages until his finger tore and bled. "Alain!" he shouted. "Alain! Those bastard Austrian dogs won't get you."

"Lay down!" commanded the young nurse who had been tending to him. She had been across the tent, but now she was rushing to him. "Don't move! You'll open your wounds."

Hallucinating, Jean didn't hear her. He was following Alain over that stone wall during the battle of Marengo and advancing on the Austrian defenses. His legs however collapsed under his weight. The muscles wouldn't respond to his commands. He tried to reach out, but his arms were just as useless. Falling, his head hit the edge of the cot, opening a wide gash on his forehead.

"Lisette, help me," called the nurse when she reached Jean. An older nurse got to her feet and hurried over. Together they lifted Jean back onto his cot. Blood seeped across his brow. The young nurse daubed the cut with the hem of her dress.

"The fool's opened his wounds again," spat Lisette impatiently. "Michelle, get the binding. We need to tie him down first."

"At least he's getting stronger. Yesterday, he wouldn't have had the strength to untie himself." She wiped sweat from her brow with the back of her hand and tried to smile bravely.

"If he keeps doing this, he'll kill himself."

Jean stared up at Lisette. Her face, red and scarred with pockmarks, scowled as she poured powdered sulfur onto his wounds and dressed them tightly with bandages one more time. "He's lucky the worst of it is his arm and leg. If the shrapnel had pierced his stomach, we couldn't help him."

Michelle brushed Jean's hair back. "He looks like such a nice boy."

Jean smiled. *Back in heaven*, he thought as he gazed at Michelle's unlined face. Michelle smiled back.

Lisette gave her a stern look. "Don't be falling for this young man. A life in the camps is not for you."

"But you do it," objected Michelle.

"I'm a fool." She turned to leave. "Go home to Paris. Return to your family. You don't belong here." They both glanced down at Jean. Lisette jutted her chin down at the boy. "If you're not careful, you'll fall for a boy like that and be following the regiment."

Michelle smiled. "Not a chance. I'm to return home when my father does."

Michelle turned to attend to other patients, while Lisette pulled a blanket up to Jean's chin.

Over the next few days, the horror within the hospital tent diminished. Wounded soldiers were either recovering, slipping quietly toward death, or had died. A routine of feeding and washing the patients, changing the sheets, and administering treatments began to take over. Twice during the week the surgeon prescribed calomel for Jean, whose wounds had become infected. Angry red stripes spread across his neck and chest. The right side of his body swelled. The wounds on his right leg had begun to ooze. Afraid he might have to amputate Jean's leg, the surgeon believed the only recourse was calomel, a mineral mixed with water to force the patient to throw up violently and experience extreme diarrhea. As the calomel supposedly purged Jean's system of poisons, he became much weaker and closer to death.

Through the nights, Michelle remained at Jean's bedside and forced him to drink warm broth. She fed him when he would wake from his delirium. She wiped his brow as he sweated his fever.

On the fourth night, Alain arrived at Jean's bedside to relieve Michelle.

"How is he?" asked Alain as he sat on the dirt floor beside Jean's cot. His left hand was wrapped in a thick bandage and was held close to his chest by a sling.

"He will live if he survives this fever," said Michelle. She wiped Jean's brow and tried to spoon a little water onto his lips. Then she glanced at Alain. "What happened to your hand?"

Alain shrugged. He held up his right hand and wiggled his thumb and index finger. "There's not much of a hand left, just two fingers." He forced a smile.

"You should be resting," replied Michelle.

"I had to make sure Jean survived." He showed no sign of leaving. "Why don't you rest, and I'll watch him."

"But your hand."

"I'm fine. It hurts a little, but that will pass." He put his good right hand on Jean's forehead. "He's the one that needs tending."

Reluctantly, but exhausted, Michelle left to sleep.

"You will make it," Alain whispered firmly to his comrade. "I promised your father." Alain spoke to the sleeping Jean through the night. He reminisced about watching Jean grow up in the camps. "Even when you were four, we knew you were something special. Your father wanted more for you than being a soldier. He knew you could do better. Me, I've never known better or worse, but your father, he could see it in you. And when your mother died—as beautiful a woman as I've ever known—even more than my Jacqueline—your father made it his duty to get you out, but then he fell, too, and died before he could keep his promise."

Alain mulled over these thoughts and finally sighed, "Now I've failed him. You're lying almost dead in a tent of men who will more likely be dead tomorrow morning. I know it, but I won't fail any more. I won't allow you to die, and you will never return to the battlefield. You must have a better life. It's the least I can do." He wiped his friend's brow with a soiled cloth.

"I will find Baron Denon. I remember he took a liking to you in Egypt. He said you have a gift and that no one draws with your sense of capturing the soul of what you're looking at. Whatever that means. I don't know."

Alain swayed half asleep as he sat on a stool beside Jean's cot. "He'll take you on. I'll pay him if I have to," he muttered.

In the shadows of the tent, Michelle lay listening to Alain. It pleased her to hear that there was something more to this boy to whom she found herself strangely attracted.

Eventually, Alain nodded off to the quiet sounds of men sleeping intermixed with occasional moans. The night nurse moved from one cot to the next checking her patients. When one woke, she tried to help him back to sleep.

In the early morning, the other nurses came on duty. It was time to feed the men and change their dressings. Jean slept through all of this, and Alain remained at his friend's side.

At midday, Michelle returned. "We're being evacuated to Paris."

"Won't that kill him?"

"No, he'll get better treatment there. The doctor thinks he's strong enough to make the trip."

Wagons pulled up beside the hospital. Wounded men who could walk made their way on their own. Those who could not were carried and placed inside the covered wagons on racks like loaves of bread. When the soldiers came to take Jean, Alain followed.

"Careful with him," said Alain. "I lost this hand saving him. I don't want you to kill him now."

"If it's God's will," answered one of porters.

"Don't get your hopes up. Half will die on the journey. It's just too hard," explained other porter.

"I won't let him." Alain climbed into the wagon behind Jean's litter.

Outside, the sun was bright. The air was still cool even though it was already late June. The ground had dried out, so the return trip through the Great St. Bernard Pass would be easier.

"Alain!" shouted Jean as he jerked awake. The train of wagons had begun to move. He tried once again to get up. "I've got to help Alain!" His eyes were wild and he fought his bindings. He was hallucinating again and could see Alain in front of him on the battlefield. His foot was mired in a man's intestines. The bloody rope of entrails wrapped around his ankle holding him standing in the belly of a dead man.

"I'm here, Jean," Alain replied. His voice quavered as he struggled to sound confident in Jean's recovery. "I'm safe."

Jean lifted his head and pain shot through him. His head fell back, and tears began to flow. "It hurts, Alain. It hurts."

"This will pass, and you'll be good as new." Alain tried to reassure him.

"Make them stop."

"They can't. I wish they could." Alain leaned in. "We're on our way back to Paris so you can heal. You'll come home with me, and my Jacqueline will make you a fine meal."

Jean breathed through gritted teeth trying to control the pain. His eyes teared under the strain.

"You'll meet Marie. She's only fifteen, but she's a fine young girl. Strong. Good teeth. You will like her." They sat in silence as the wagon rocked on its way up the pass.

After a while, Jean turned his head toward Alain and for the first time noticed his bandaged hand. "What happened?"

"Oh, a scratch is all."

"Let me see."

Alain held out the stump revealing that most of his left hand was gone. Since his hand had not been dressed in days, the tattered bandage had slipped away and the raw, angry wound peaked out. "It's healing well. And I still have my thumb and index finger. That's enough to hold a mug of cognac."

Jean tried to smile.

"I won't leave you again. I've lost my heart in this war. I won't be going back."

"But you've been with Napoleon since the beginning," whispered Jean. He had never heard Alain express doubt. "You've always said you'll be with him until you're buried."

"Why are we attacking the Austrians and Italians? What have they ever done to us?"

"France is a great nation!" answered Jean forcefully. "We are destined to rule the world. This is Napoleon's destiny, no?" In the back of his mind he knew he could never admit to the war's futility. Otherwise, it would be admitting to the senselessness of his parents' death. Though they didn't die on the battlefield, they died in the camps of an army on the move.

Alain mussed Jean's hair. "Of course." His words could not disguise the look of defeat in his face.

CHAPTER 5

A Paris Hospital

"Hmmm, not bad."

Jean did not bother to look up. His pencil scraped along the rough page with a quickness and ease that revealed remarkable skill. "It's just practice." The confidence in each line gave weight and volume where only compressed lead dust adhered.

"No, I mean that's really good. Where'd you learn to do that?" asked Michelle, the nurse who had been in the battlefield hospital. She leaned against the same windowsill Jean's sketch pad was propped against. Michelle and Jean stood at the end of a large ward for amputees at Boisvert Military Hospital, in the middle of Paris. She had returned at the same time as Jean.

The pencil in Jean's hand moved fluidly. It captured with remarkable skill and vitality the newly constructed building along the street outside the window. "I was assigned to the engraver Baron Dominique Vivant Denon to assist him on Napoleon's Egyptian campaign."

"The baron?"

"Yes," replied Jean. "You know him?" He didn't even look up. Instead he focused on the tall, six-story buildings that appeared in more and more detail with each stroke of the pencil. By moving his hand downward in a quick motion, he articulated the mansard roofs along the skyline.

"Everyone does," said Michelle. "He is a great friend of Jacques-Louis David. In fact, David even saved the baron's life during the Revolution when his belongings were confiscated and he was placed on the list of the proscribed."

"The proscribed?"

"Yes, those who were sentenced to have their heads chopped off by the guillotine."

"It's good he didn't die," Jean said inanely. Then he wanted to kick himself for sounding so stupid.

Michelle pointed at the drawing. "Is this what you want to do?" she asked, changing the subject.

Jean shrugged and paused. He looked at her. What he wanted to do was kiss her, but he didn't. "I guess, but I don't really know." He stared down at his hands. "The baron had promised to help me if I made it to Paris. I want to contact him, but I've been too scared. My dream is that maybe I can become an apprentice in his studio."

"You'll have to wait," said Michelle. "The baron is not due back to Paris for at least a month."

"How would you know?"

"You hear things out on the street," Michelle said with a smile. "Which reminds me. You should be walking more. And now that Napoleon is rebuilding the city, this is the best time to be walking. Amazing new buildings and sculptures are springing up on every corner."

"But I don't know if they'll let me, with all the work to be done on the ward." Though several months had passed since Jean was wounded, he still lived at the hospital, but no longer as a patient. He was now an orderly on the amputee ward. He spent his days changing bandages and making beds. Michelle was also assigned to this ward, which pleased Jean. He loved spending time with her.

Jean tore the page from his pad and set it on the windowsill. On the new white page, he drew dark wide curves. In a moment, the image of a face began to emerge. After a few more strokes, the face of Alain became clear. Jean drew him laughing. As the cheeks rose in mirth, the eyes crinkled.

"I can see you're *working* hard."

"Well, not *exactly* now," said Jean. "The doctor hasn't made his rounds."

"Look what you've done."

As he lifted his sketch pad, he saw a deep gouge in his paper where his pencil had dug in.

"Sorry."

Jean shrugged. "It's just marks on a page, anyway."

Michelle took the sketch pad from him. "You've got talent," said Michelle as she examined the drawings in the book. There were many sketches of buildings and people throughout the pages, but Michelle stopped when she turned to a page with a portrait of herself. "Oh, Jean! This is so wonderful. You make me look so much better."

"I could never capture how beautiful you really are." Jean flushed at the sounds of his words. "God, I sound like a moron."

"May I keep it?"

Jean ripped the page from his sketch pad. "Take it."

"You forgot to sign it!"

Jean flushed again. He didn't really think his work was worth signing.

"You should stay in Paris," insisted Michelle. "With this talent, you should be studying in David's studio, not dying on the battlefield."

There was a cryptic look in her eyes.

"Maybe I was lucky, but the army is what I know and it's where I should return."

Michelle bowed her head. She struggled to speak. "I'm not so sure war, any war, is worth it," she said.

Jean's eyes flashed. "You can't mean that. France is destined to rule. We are right, and if we don't seize the moment, some other country will." He played for a moment with his pencil. "That last battle proved that I was a good soldier. I was afraid, but I didn't hesitate. I can do that again. It will be much easier next time."

"Maybe so, but what about these men?" She moved her arm in a wide sweep to include the dozens of soldiers with missing limbs who were lying in the ward. "They'll be lucky if they don't starve when they're discharged from the hospital. All they have to look forward to is becoming beggars on the streets. They were brave, too. They didn't run. And look at them. Do you want that to happen to you?"

"I know I'm lucky," Jean whispered. He reached down and rubbed his leg. He was surprised at how stiff and difficult it was for him to do the simplest things. Just walking down a flight of stairs would leave him out of breath. He could not fully extend his right arm, but that wasn't a problem since he was left-handed. Sharp, shooting pain would radiate down his calf if he turned too quickly. He could feel pieces of shrapnel floating under the skin in his legs. On particularly wet, rainy nights his leg would ache deep in the bone. "I'll live a pretty good life, and these men won't. I know that."

The two stood by the window looking out at the street for what seemed like a while.

Finally, Jean sighed. "Now Alain says he going back, and I can't let him go. If he died…" His voice trailed off.

"I know." Michelle put her hand on his arm. It was like a warm current had suddenly begun to flow through him. "You must learn to paint," she said emphatically.

Jean felt her breath on his neck and shivered. He turned his head toward her and smiled. He had come to appreciate Michelle's company over the last few months, but now was aware of a feeling he had not expected. It was more than just friendship. It felt deeper. He wanted to speak to her of it, but he held back. It wasn't just that he did not have words for what he felt. It was also that he was afraid of discovering. Unconsciously, he had made a decision never to ask. It was as if knowing would destroy any possibility of their falling in love. Deep down he was afraid his feelings could not survive the harsh light of reality. As he recovered, he always turned the conversation away from their pasts.

Gently. Hesitantly. He placed his hand over hers. He did not want to lose her and so did not want to risk anything that would put their friendship in danger. For Jean, that meant possibly finding out that Michelle really was a camp girl much like the Egyptian Christian woman Manal with whom he and a number of other soldiers had slept with. He had enjoyed those quick encounters, but could hear his mother's disapproving voice echo in his head every time he visited Manal. Besides the wives of soldiers like his mother, women like Manal were just about the only women he had ever come in contact with.

It sounded so trite to him as he recalled his mother's words in his mind. She had warned him about camp girls, and so he had been afraid to know too much about Michelle. Otherwise, his mother's warnings might be confirmed, and unconsciously he did not want that to happen. In an army camp, almost any woman or girl who was not married was a prostitute or the child of a prostitute who would eventually become a whore herself. It was not much of a life, but for many women without husbands it was the only way to earn money to survive. He remembered his mother's harsh words for these women. He could still hear his mother's tone when she called them "more deadly than the battlefield." He did not want to learn that Michelle fell in this category and so stayed as far away as possible from discovering whether it was true or not.

"How would you know about something like this?" Jean asked, surprised that she would have an opinion about art.

"Oh, I know more than just how to take care of soldiers," replied Michelle teasingly.

They stood there in awkward silence for a moment. Jean wanted something more, but he just didn't know exactly what that *more* was.

"Well, if you can find the time, the doctor needs your help." She turned quickly and strode down the center aisle between the long rows of beds.

Still feeling her warm skin on the tips of his fingers, Jean watched her walk away. He liked her confident stride, and he noticed how even when she simply brushed a strand of hair from her face, it was attractive. He wondered what her brown hair would look like if it were loose and falling onto her shoulders, but he tried to quickly erase such thoughts from his mind. His mother's warning still echoed telling him to keep his distance.

"Jean!" shouted Dr. Rousseau. "I need help turning this patient."

Jean set aside his pencil and pad. "Coming!" Jean limped down the ward.

As they lifted the patient to slide a fresh sheet under him, Dr. Rousseau muttered, "This is so pointless."

"What?" asked Jean.

"These men lying here. If we hadn't gone to war, they'd be home tending their fields and raising families. Instead, they will live a life of pain and dependence."

Jean was embarrassed to hear the doctor express these thoughts. He tried to reason that such a learned man would understand much better than Jean ever would how important the empire was not just to the citizens of France, but to the citizens of the world. "But what about freedom and liberty? Isn't that why we're fighting? To free the rest of Europe from the tyranny of kings? Isn't that the destiny of the French Republic?"

Dr. Rousseau looked up and stared at Jean for a moment as if he were making some sort of calculation about how he should respond. Finally, he sighed and said without conviction, "You're right. Napoleon is leading us to a better world." He pulled up the patient's blanket and tucked it in. "And returning France to greatness."

Jean hesitated to speak again. He was confused by the doctor's contradictory statements, but was relieved to have the doctor affirm the truths Jean had been told his entire life. Still, in the back of his mind, a small bit of doubt festered.

Later that afternoon, Jean sought out Michelle. They sat at the top of the stairs drinking hot tea.

"I'm not so sure Dr. Rousseau supports Napoleon," he said as he blew steam off his cup.

"Why would he?" replied Michelle. "He's a doctor."

"He's also French."

"I'm not following you."

"It is every Frenchman's duty to support the Republic," explained Jean.

"Even if the Republic is wrong?" asked Michelle.

"The Republic is never wrong," replied Jean firmly, but as he spoke these words he knew how foolish he sounded. "What I mean is France will be destroyed if we don't hold strong."

Michelle pointed with her chin toward the amputee ward. "And those men are worth the sacrifice?"

Through the doors Jean could see the rows of suffering.

"What about you? Your wounds are worth it?" pressed Michelle.

"I wouldn't still be here if they weren't," he said quietly. He then swirled the tea around in his cup. Neither spoke for a few minutes.

"Jean." Michelle put her hand on his arm. "Imagine what it's like for a doctor like Rousseau, who only sees ruined lives. Whatever he does, those men will never be whole again. Big abstract words like 'liberty' and 'freedom' won't put their shattered lives back together."

After a moment, Jean blew out his breath and nodded. "I guess I can understand Dr. Rousseau's doubt," he conceded.

"And remember, he doesn't run away," Michelle added. "He might have doubts at times, but he stays and treats these men."

Jean had to admit that even he had doubts at times, especially during the worst of it. "Even Alain has said he hates war, but he goes back to fight. He doesn't run either." Jean smiled at Michelle. He took her hand in his. "Actions speak more than any words ever could."

"And Dr. Rousseau is the same."

"I just wish I was with Alain and not stuck here in this hospital."

"Oh, and so you hate the company?" She pulled her hand from his.

"No! That's not what I meant at all. I really like—well—like working with you," added Jean somewhat flustered. "It's just that here in Paris, safely away from the front lines, people don't really understand how much danger France is in."

"I'd miss you if you left," added Michelle quietly.

Jean stood. "I've got to check on the ward."

"Easy now, Private," said a captain who had had both legs blown off by an artillery shell. Jean was turning the officer so he could slide a bed pan underneath him.

"Don't worry I've got you," replied Jean as he propped the captain up. After so many weeks working with amputees, Jean knew how off balance men who had recently lost their legs could be. They were now so top heavy that they flipped over easily. As Jean came around the bed to position the captain on the bed pan, he spoke again, "Can I ask you something?"

"Sure."

"Well, you said that you outlived two wives."

"That's right."

"So you know something about women?"

"Oh, you've got women troubles."

Jean nodded.

"Is it with that beauty over there?" Michelle was at the other end of the ward attending to another patient.

"Well, I grew up in the army and…" Jean didn't have words for what he wanted to say. "I'm kind of—how do you know?" Jean could not finish his thought.

"There only one way to know," replied the grizzled captain.

"How that?" said Jean.

"You ask." The captain laughed, merriment rising in his eyes.

"Oh." Jean didn't know what to say. The thought of asking Michelle if she liked him seemed more frightening that charging the Austrian artillery at Marengo.

The afternoon quickly fell into the routine that Jean had come to expect on the ward. He moved up and down the rows helping wherever he was needed. He carried soiled sheets to the laundry. He returned with fresh bandages. He dressed wounds and fed patients, and he forgot the uncertainty of the morning.

As evening approached, he watched Michelle putting on her coat. Jean wanted to help her with the coat, but he was suddenly shy. He had not had time to speak to her since their conversation earlier. Now that he had the opportunity, he couldn't think of what to say.

Fortunately, Michelle spoke first.

"Jean, I almost forgot." She crossed the ward to him. She was reaching into the pocket of her coat. "I bought this for you." She held out an inkwell and feather pen. "I thought you might like to try drawing in ink, instead of just pencil and charcoal."

Jean hesitated and looked down. He wasn't sure if he should accept her gift, but didn't know how not to.

"Go on," she pressed. "It won't bite you." She held out the gifts.

"Thank…thank you," he said, trying not to touch her hand as he reached out for it.

"See you tomorrow." She waved and was gone before Jean could say anything further.

"Michelle, would…." He wanted to ask her to dinner or to go for a walk or simply to talk just a moment longer, but courage failed him. The captain made it sound so simple, but the actual action seemed impossible.

Michelle turned back.

"Thank you," he said simply.

"Yes." She stood there for a moment as if expecting him to say something more. Then she departed.

"I can charge a line of Austrian riflemen, but I can't ask a simple girl to coffee," he muttered. "Coward." He thought he could still smell her perfume floating through the ward. He decided then that he would not let an opportunity like this slip by again.

CHAPTER 6

The Painter of the Revolution

"Look, Jean!" Michelle leaned out the third-floor window of the hospital ward. The early morning light barely kissed the dewy cobblestones as she watched two plainly dressed figures enter the narrow street, followed by a retinue of elaborately uniformed soldiers.

"It's him! Napoleon!" gasped Jean as his eyes scoured the street. "I've seen him before. I'd know him anywhere. But who's that with him?" He turned to hug Michelle in his excitement, but then froze when he realized what he was doing. All night, he had worried that she might not return to the ward this morning, that perhaps her gift was really a good-bye present, that he would never see her again, just when he was beginning to care about her. In the army, he had never really had time to think about girls beyond just wanting to have sex with them. Now, thoughts of Michelle crowded out everything else. He wanted to spend all his time with her. Just be around her. To hold her hand.

"Jacques-Louis David."

"Really? How do you know?" Jean thought he might explode with excitement.

"I've met him," Michelle said.

Jean stared at Michelle for a moment. "You?"

"Why not? Lots of people have met David."

Jean nodded. "I, too, know a friend of his." Even though he had already discussed the baron with her, he felt the need to mention him one more time.

"He's going to introduce me to him," he added, trying to impress her. "The baron, I mean."

Michelle smiled. "I think they're coming here."

"They look…" Jean hesitated to say.

"What?" asked Michelle.

"Well—so average."

Michelle laughed.

For a second, Jean though she was laughing at him. Anger flashed as he tried to explain himself. "I mean they're two of the most powerful people in France, and they look like stable hands. You wouldn't even notice them if it weren't for the uniformed guards."

First Consul Napoleon Bonaparte and the painter of the revolution, Jacques-Louis David, climbed the stairs to the hospital and entered. They were followed by a crowd of well-dressed men and Napoleon's guards.

Jean ran down the corridor between the beds in the ward and dashed into the hallway. He leaned over the stair's railing to get another glimpse of the two.

Michelle followed. Without looking down the stairwell, she said, "I think they're coming up here."

"Oh, I hope so." Jean couldn't contain himself. He had been living and working on this ward for months with hardly a break. "I've been meaning to visit the Louvre since I've been here, but haven't been able to get away."

"I want to go with you," said Michelle as she and Jean watched the two great men ascend.

Michelle's response thrilled Jean. "I did get to see *The Intervention of the Sabine Women*," said Jean. "It cost me a franc and two centimes, but it was worth it."

"I heard that David began the *Sabines* when he was imprisoned —"

"Me, too," interrupted Jean. He so wanted to impress her with his knowledge of art. "I couldn't believe he painted the soldiers in the…" he hesitated.

"Nude," inserted Michelle.

Jean stared at Michelle. Her vulgarity surprised him, but then he suspected that she was probably the child of a camp whore, if not one herself.

"Yes, everyone was scandalized," she continued, "but David argued that it was essential to portray the soldiers the way the Greeks did."

"How do you know that?'

"My father told me."

"Your father?"

Before she could explain, the entire hospital erupted in cheers. Doctors and nurses from the other wards crowded the hallways surrounding the stairs.

Caught up in the excitement, Jean shouted "Here they come!" The two men passed the second-floor landing and began to climb to the third floor. As Napoleon and David approached, Jean was stunned by their appearance. He realized they weren't simply average, but strange. Napoleon was dressed in a corporal's great coat. His boots needed shining, and he was hatless. David wore a shabby coat that desperately needed cleaning, a yellowing white shirt with stains, and a carelessly knotted necktie. Their clothing however was only the half of it. The right side of David's face was lopsided. A large tumor protruded, creating a lump on the side of his face. It pulled his lip down so that when he spoke it appeared that half of his face was frozen in some sort of sad grimace.

Napoleon on the other hand had a face that was the opposite of frozen. He had so many tics that he seemed always in motion. Every few moments, his left eye would wink and then his nose would twitch. Jean tried not to stare at the two. He bit his lip so he would not laugh. As he glanced over at Michelle, her eyes danced as she stared at them.

Jean pulled Michelle away from the railing. "We better make sure the ward is in order. This is too important to be embarrassed." Michelle nodded, and the two hurried back in to straightened the patients' linens.

The air seemed to change when Napoleon and David crossed the threshold into the ward. To Jean's surprise, he was more excited about seeing David than Napoleon. He had gotten a glimpse of the First Consul at the start of the Marengo campaign, riding a mule just outside Val d'Etremont, but he had never seen David in person before. He had just heard stories about his great talent from his teacher and friend, the baron.

"It really doesn't matter," said Napoleon as he strode purposefully into the ward. The two men seemed to be in a heated discussion. Behind them, several men flowed into the room and began setting up drawing tables.

This caught Jean's attention. He moved over to the drawing tables and saw two men, one old and the other young, laying out paper and pens. "What are your doing?" asked Jean.

"We're here to record Napoleon's visit," the young man answered rather curtly. He started drawing the shape of the room and filling the space with beds. The older man drew quick sketches of Napoleon and David, along with the guards in their elaborate uniforms.

Over on the other side of the ward, David seemed upset. "I can't do it unless you sit for me." Napoleon and David paced the length of the ward and turned. Napoleon had his arms crossed and a stubborn look on his face, though this was hard to detect since his facial tics masked other expressions.

"You went off to Egypt just when I was halfway done with your portrait and so never finished it." David threw up his hands. "I have only a face floating on a canvas with no body."

"The accuracy of the portrait is of no importance," Napoleon announced dismissively. "I want you to paint history, not me."

"I don't understand."

Jean stood by the two men who were drawing. "Is this for an engraving?"

"Yes, in this week's edition of *Liberté*," answered the older man. "Now, please, we don't have time to talk. We need to work."

Jean left the men and saw that Napoleon had stopped in front of Lieutenant Alois, a soldier who had lost both legs at Marengo. Jean remembered hearing how the lieutenant had saved five men and killed twenty Austrians while being wounded in both legs. He almost bled to death on the battlefield, but he had cauterized his own wounds with gunpowder.

"Is this the soldier?" asked Napoleon.

Doctor Rousseau hurried up. "Yes, your excellency."

In the corner, the artists drew frantically.

Napoleon held out his hand. A soldier from his guard gave him a small wooden box. Inside was a medal, which the First Consul extracted.

Still wrapped up in their argument, David did not even notice that Napoleon had moved on. "I need..."

The First Consul waved for David to be silent and then spoke, "By the powers vested in me by the Republic of France, I bestow upon you..." He glanced over at the soldier.

"Lieutenant Ricard," the doctor supplied.

"Lieutenant Ricard," repeated Napoleon, "the Crois de Guerre for your heroics during battle." The First Consul pinned the medal to the bed sheet. Lieutenant Ricard was not awake to receive the award. Jean knew that he would probably never awake again, so the medal would eventually go to his next of kin.

"It's not important to portray what I look like, but what I represent," explained Napoleon as if their conversation had not been interrupted at all by the award ceremony. He immediately went over to the temporary drawing tables, which had been set up. He watched the artists continue to draw the scene. "This is to be in the newspaper?"

"Yes, First Consul," answered the older man.

Napoleon's face twitched as he stared at the artists working. Then he pointed at the portrayal of himself. "Make sure you have me in uniform with a bicorn."

The older man nodded. "Of course, First Consul."

Napoleon then turned back to David who had also been watching the men draw. "Now, where were we?"

"You need to sit for your portrait," said David.

Napoleon began shaking his head. "My soul, my spirit, not my physical details. That is what is important, not a perfect likeness of me."

"But I need you to paint you," insisted David. "How else can I capture your soul. Otherwise, it will be someone else's soul." Like a pouting child, he followed Napoleon out of the ward and back into the hallway.

Napoleon turned and took the painter by the arm. "Listen one last time, Jacques. It is of no importance whether I sit for the portrait or not. No one knows if portraits of great men are likenesses: it suffices that genius lives. Paint my character, not my likeness. Paint my genius. Alexander the Great certainly did not pose for Apelles." Napoleon was referring to the famous portrait of Alexander the Great.

David hung his head, beaten. "You might be right, but I would argue that the painting would have been even greater if he had had Alexander standing there for the portrait."

Napoleon dismissed David's argument with a wave of his hand. The men moved on to the next ward.

Michelle followed, calling back to Jean, "I'll be right back. I forgot something." She disappeared into the ward where Napoleon and David had gone.

Jean didn't really notice. He was too wrapped up in the work of the engravers. "When do you start the engraving?"

"When we return to the studio."

"Will it be copper?" Jean had learned to engrave from the baron.

"Yes."

"I studied with Baron Dominique Vivant Denon."

The older man looked up and surveyed Jean. "Yes, of course you did," he said in disbelief.

"No, really," protested Jean.

"Go away," replied the engraver. "I don't have time to listen to such nonsense."

A moment later, Michelle returned with an armful of sheets.

"Let's start changing the dressings," she said, breaking the spell the two great men had cast over the room.

Jean hesitated. He felt like a fool because these artists didn't believe him. He wanted to show them his sketchbook to prove that he could draw, but he knew that he'd make a bigger fool of himself if he did that. He would seem desperate, and nobody believes someone who is desperate. Reluctantly turning away from the artists working, Jean went over to the cabinet and picked up a stack of bandages. Together, Jean and Michelle worked on a soldier by the door who had lost his arm just below the elbow. The man was in great pain, but if they wrapped the bandages tightly the pain lessened considerably.

"Aggggghhhhh," the soldier moaned. "My hand. My hand is killing me!" By now Jean knew that phantom pain from a missing limb was common. The soldier was delirious from fever. Jean was not even certain if the man would live. The amputation had been successful, but more often than not the recovery killed the patient.

"Him!"

Jean ignored the shouting. Patients shouted all the time.

"I want that boy!"

Jean looked up.

"Yes, you!"

Jean saw Jacques-Louis David pointing directly at him.

Both engravers stopped their work and looked up.

Across the aisle standing beside another bed, Michelle looked up and smiled.

"Me?"

"Yes, I want you to be at my studio first thing in the morning. You will sit for my portrait of Napoleon."

Speechless, Jean stared as David turned and disappeared into the hall.

CHAPTER 7

A Brief Meeting

"Did you hear?"

"Yes, Jean, I heard."

"Do you think he meant me?"

"Yes, Jean, he did."

"Maybe he was pointing at someone else."

"No. He was pointing right at you."

Jean sat down on the edge of a bed. "His studio is in the Louvre." He glanced over at the two engravers, who were now packing up.

"I know."

"How do you know?"

"I have to go," Michelle suddenly said. "Meet me at the Café Violin this evening."

Jean stared at her for a moment. *Who is this girl?* Jean wondered. *I've known her for eight months and still don't know a thing about her.* He wanted to celebrate, and he wanted to do it with Michelle, but the voice of his mother warning him made him hesitate. "I don't know if I can get away."

"You have a new job. You don't have to stay in the ward any longer."

"Yes, you're right," he hesitated, "but I need to get ready."

"Meet me, please. I have a surprise." Michelle stiffened.

Jean agree, more excited than he was willing to admit.

That evening, Jean strolled along the streets. He enjoyed the crowds going in and out of restaurants. With the Café Violin just around the corner, Jean realized he had spent the afternoon thinking about Michelle. Over the past few months, they had spent most of their time together either focused on his recovery or working in the ward. She had volunteered almost nothing about her past while he had told her his life story. Tonight, he vowed to finally find out everything about her no matter how much she resisted.

As he turned the corner, he saw the café ahead. An array of tables were set up across the sidewalk out front. Only one table was taken. Two people, a fashionably dressed man and woman, sat together talking and laughing. Jean smiled. He thought it was wonderful that two people could enjoy each other so. The woman had her back to him, so he couldn't see how she was responding, but he assumed it must be going well because she had just accepted a bouquet of flowers. The woman's face was hidden by the blossoms.

As he approached, Jean scanned the café for Michelle, but the small place had only these two customers. Then he noticed something familiar about the elegantly dressed woman whose back was to him. Her hair looked like Michelle's, but that couldn't be her. At least he thought it couldn't. Where would she get such wonderful clothes?

At that moment, the woman turned and looked over her shoulder. The woman smiled at him. It was a wonderful smile. Jean was stunned when he realized the woman *was* Michelle. Dressed in the most exquisite pale blue silk dress, she stood and held out her hand to Jean.

With the realization that this beautiful woman was Michelle, Jean blanched. He had made a terrible error and miscalculated completely who she was. In that instant, Jean knew he was out of his depth, and this put him on edge. For months, he had been talking to her like she was some common girl who followed the army from camp to camp. He had been so certain of her origins that he had never bothered to inquire. Michelle must have known, but she had done nothing to correct him.

Suddenly, Jean wanted to turn and run away. For the second time that day he felt like a complete fool. She was probably playing with him by not telling him who she was. He didn't like not being in control. He was a soldier, not a child.

"Jean!" She waved him over.

The young man with her stood and bowed slightly. His thick, long brown hair was pulled back in a ponytail, tied back by a black velvet ribbon.

"This is Jules."

The man held out his hand. "A pleasure." His build was much slighter than Jean's and he stood a good three inches shorter.

Jean automatically shook it, but he could not take his eyes off of Michelle.

Michelle seemed to flush.

He wasn't expecting someone else to be with her, and this angered him. He had assumed it would be just the two of them, and he felt betrayed by her apparent deception. But he knew better than to say something. Just wait, he told himself, and see what happens.

"Thank you, Jean. Please sit." She gave a graceful wave of her hand toward the empty chair at the table.

The man named Jules scowled. He seemed no older than Jean. In an absurd flash of insecurity, Jean sized Jules up and decided that he could definitely take him in a fight.

"Waiter! Cognac, please," Jules called rather imperiously.

Jean took an immediate dislike to this man. He tried to speak, but his tongue felt thick and immobile.

"It is so nice to see you," Michelle said politely. "I am so happy that you came."

Jean nodded dumbly, still unable to say a word. He was speechless before her beauty.

The waiter set a snifter of cognac on the table. Jules swallowed the amber liquid quickly and spoke rather aggressively, "So you're a soldier."

Jean eyed the young man warily. "Yes."

"Those silly uniforms make good targets for the enemy."

Jean laughed, trying to make a joke of it all. "But not as good a target as the red coats of the Austrians. You can see them even in the dark."

"Cannon fodder." Jules waved to the waiter for another round.

"Jules, no," protested Michelle as she put a hand on the young man's arm.

"That's all soldiers are good for," said Jules heatedly. "Napoleon has a hundred, no, a thousand idiots just like you killed every day."

"Napoleon cares very much about the army," Jean replied rather sharply. "He doesn't waste his men."

Jules snorted. "Parisians see through the little fool. He is full of hot air. No educated person would ever follow this peasant into battle."

"That's why lazy cowards like you were executed along with the royal family," spat Jean. "If Napoleon heard you speak such treason, you'd be guillotined at dawn."

"Don't insult me! If anyone deserves to die, it's fools like you who put on the uniform."

Jean stiffened. Suddenly, this was no longer a little argument between two men for the attentions of a woman. Memories of comrades falling in battle around him rushed into Jean's consciousness. Somehow their memory and sacrifice were at stake.

"Cannon fodder!" he repeated, pointing his finger in Jean's face. Jean smacked it away.

Crash! The table turned as Jean stood to defend himself. The flowers spilled across the sidewalk. "If it's a fight you want, then let's go." He raised his fists and started toward Jules, but Michelle stepped between the two.

"Please, I didn't bring you two together for this!"

"Well, you'll have to try to restrain your paramour's rudeness in the future!" Angrily, Jean turned to leave. Then he stopped. "Whatever you wanted Michelle, I guess it wasn't really important." Jean strode down the street.

"Wait," Michelle called after him.

Jean was beyond anger, but not just at Jules. He was more enraged at himself for so misreading Michelle. "How could you have deceived me so? You're no better than this overdressed…" He tried to think of the right word. "Peacock!"

As he marched away, Jean chastised himself, "How could I have been so stupid to like her." He slammed his fist against his thigh in frustration. "She's just a rich girl who spent a few months slumming."

Into the night, Jean raged and wandered. One moment, he'd imagine arguing with Michelle. In another moment he'd see himself leveling Jules. Next, he would be filled with anticipation about arriving at David's studio.

"The Louvre! My God!" he shouted. Then his pace quickened as if he were trying to outrun all that happened earlier this evening.

As if on a merry-go-round, these thoughts raced through his mind over and over again until he found himself at the door to a tavern. He could hear the singing and carousing inside. Suddenly, he felt the need to be around people. He opened the door and was almost knocked back by the smell of tobacco and spilt beer.

"Ho! A soldier!" shouted the barmaid as he entered. She was a fat woman with one brown tooth poking from her jaw. Her greasy hair was flattened against her skull, and her hands were nearly black as coal.

"Let me buy you a drink," a man standing with his friends called to Jean. The men smelled of rotting flesh.

Jean straightened with pride. These people recognized a soldier and respected him.

The barmaid placed a mug of beer before him, and Jean took a deep swallow. "Thank you."

Jean stood at the bar and drank alone, turning down an invitation to join the malodorous men. By his third beer, he was feeling much better. He had forgotten the early evening and was full of excitement and anticipation.

He leaned back against the bar and scanned the crowded room. He tried to imagine how he would capture such a scene with his pen. He tried to choose which details were key and which were just background. After a while, a woman leaned against him. He could feel her soft breasts against his chest. "Care to buy a thirsty girl a drink?" Her breath stank of rotting teeth and beer.

To his own surprise, Jean agreed and pulled out his purse. He tossed a few coins on the bar and waved to the barmaid for two more beers. When the mugs arrived, the woman drank hers in one long swallow and banged her mug back down on the bar.

"Thirsty, eh?" asked Jean.

"Sure," she slurred.

Jean wasn't sure why he was doing this, but he ordered another beer for his new companion. They drank into the night until Jean was ready to leave. Somehow, the woman convinced him to walk her home.

That was the last thing he remembered before he woke lying in a pool of his own vomit. His coat was ripped down the back. His pockets were turned out and his head ached. A trickle of blood ran down his forehead into his eyes. Dizzy, he clawed at a lamppost to right himself. It was still night, and he recognized the street. He was only a couple of blocks from the hospital. After making sure nothing was broken, he stumbled down the street.

CHAPTER 8

A Friend Indeed

"Who is that?" Jean lingered at the end of the block. The entrance to the hospital was several hundred feet farther down the street. After a night of drinking and being mugged, he was not ready for a fight.

A hulking, menacing shape was curled up on the hospital steps, which the dim lamplight did not illuminate beyond its immense size and shape.

Slowly, Jean limped down the block.

"Maybe it's a dead horse," he muttered. Horses often expired on the streets and were left to rot until the city hauled the carcass away. "No, it's some kind of human." He stopped to consider the risk to himself. This person was clearly much bigger than he was, and in his injured state he was not in a condition to fight. "Maybe I should find a park bench and wait until morning comes." He took a few more steps toward the bulk. "I could go straight to David's studio. I shouldn't even be coming back here to the hospital."

Beaten, robbed, he felt the treacherousness of the city surround him. And, even Michelle, the person he cared about most after Alain, had betrayed him. She had nursed him in his recovery. She had encouraged his drawing and praised his work. She had given him a pen and ink to draw. She had even asked to keep a portrait of her that he had drawn. But tonight. *Tonight*! raged Jean. Though unfounded, he felt that she had deceived and humiliated him.

"Why did she have to bring *him* along," he muttered. "I thought she liked me, but she seemed to be playing me for a fool." He glanced at the hospital up the street. "I don't belong in David's studio at the Louvre any more than I belong at the dinner table with the Pope." In his mind, Michelle and that dreadful Jules had turned on him because he was a soldier. This evening's disaster made him question whether he was really ready to leave the safety of the hospital.

"But this isn't my home either," he said bitterly, remembering that Michelle worked in the hospital with him. "I don't want to see her ever again." Jean staggered forward. "I should just go back to the regiment. That's where I belong." He stomped his leg on the side-walk. Pain shot up his thigh. "It's good enough. Alain went back with worse." He was thinking how Alain had returned to the regiment with half a hand. "Paris is for the rich. I'm a soldier," he repeated as if trying to convince himself that what he really wanted to do was not work in David's studio and learn to become an artist, but to soldier in Napoleon's army. "I was brought up in the army, and it's all I know."

With a sense of determination, Jean now approached the hospital. He decided he was going to refuse the assignment to David's studio and insist on returning to the army. That's where he belonged, he repeated in his mind. "Let me just find the duty officer."

Suddenly, the shadowy figure rose. Standing several steps above him, the beast towered over Jean, ready to pounce, but just as quickly every muscle in Jean's body relaxed. The pale light had finally landed on what was clearly a man.

"Jean!" Alain spread his arms to embrace the boy. Jean staggered up the steps and nearly fell. Alain caught him. "My God! What happened to you?"

"Got into a little trouble." He tried to laugh.

"Let's get you inside."

"It's just a cut. I'm all right. I'm just tired."

Alain held Jean at arms length and examined him. "Let me take you home and get some hot stew in you. Jacqueline has some on the stove left over from supper."

Jean tried to protest, but he was too tired. "When did you get back?"

"Shhh," Alain whispered. "We'll talk once we've cleaned you up and gotten food in your stomach." Alain guided him down the street and across town.

It felt good to be wrapped in Alain's safe and powerful embrace.

Alain and his family lived in a slum along a sewer that at one time was a winding brook that emptied into the Seine River, which ran through the center of Paris. The building was a ramshackle wooden tenement that looked as if a slight breeze could destroy it. As the two climbed the rickety stairs to the second-floor apartment, Jean thought the steps might collapse beneath them. They were split and corroded with grime. A baby's cry came from an apartment on the first floor. Someone began shouting for the child to shut up. Then there was a sound of a smack across a face.

Silence. It lasted a mere moment, but felt like an eternity for Jean.

Finally, a wale erupted even more fiercely.

"Ignore those animals on the first floor. We'll all be out in two months time anyway."

"Out?"

"Yes, the building's been condemned. They're going to build a grand boulevard right through here."

"But why?" asked Jean.

"Napoleon needs some place for his army to march," Alain replied bitterly. "In a year's time we'll be standing in the middle of a cobblestone street."

"Where will Jacqueline and the children go?"

"To the streets, maybe. I'm thinking about having them travel with the army."

Jean nodded. He knew what a hard life that was since that was how he grew up. "But you have a daughter. You don't want her growing up in the camps."

"No, that wouldn't be good." He shrugged and fished a skeleton key out of his pocket. He unlocked the door and shouted, "I'm home, and look who I drug out of the gutter."

The room was dark. A lamp turned low sat in the middle of a small table casting very little illumination. What Jean could make out was that the apartment was just one room. A stove stood in one corner, with a bed beside it. Above the stove hung a shelf with a few plates, pots, and various cooking utensils. The only other adornment on the wall was a cross. The table had two chairs arranged around it. Against the wall stood a roughly constructed armoire and a wooden crate that Jean recognized as one of the boxes in which muskets were shipped.

Jean heard the sound of movement in the room before he saw its source. A woman who looked at least a decade older than Alain sat up in the bed. The woman's hair was tangled, and she had been sleeping in her clothes. Her face was deeply lined.

"Come on, Marie." She was shaking a lump beside her. "Get up."

The lump turned and moaned. At the other end of the bed the heads of two small boys popped up.

"Papa!" The boys leaped from the bed and ran to their father.

Alain kneeled and wrapped both boys in his arms. Jean watched from the doorway, glad to feel safe. The only homes he had ever been in—that he could remember—had been ransacked by soldiers. Their occupants were at best cowering in a corner, and at worst dead. To drink in the love that this small one-room apartment held was a revelation to him. It was something he never had with his mother following his father in the military camps across Europe. It was also something that he never imagined he would have himself, but it was something that he now he desperately wanted.

"We were afraid you had left for good without saying good-bye," cried the younger of the two boys.

"Never!" growled Alain as he buried the boy's head in his beard.

As Alain hugged his boys, Jacqueline got out of bed and turned up the lamp so that more light filled the room. Then she stoked the fire in the stove with a piece of coal. "You must be hungry."

At that moment, the lump in the bed became a young woman. She stepped out of the bed and wrapped her arms around her father.

Looking over his children's shoulders, Alain said, "Jean, that beautiful woman by the stove is Jacqueline. She is the beauty I have been telling you about."

"Welcome, Jean," beamed Jacqueline. "You must already know that Alain is one of the worst liars in the world."

"Now, come meet my little ones," said Alain.

Jean smiled and entered the apartment.

"This is Girard." Alain patted the smallest on the head. "He'll be six next month."

Jean shook the boy's hand.

"This is Alain, named after me. He is ten." Jean took that boy's hand and noticed that he was small for his age, not much bigger than his younger brother.

"And this is the apple of my eye, Marie. She just turned fifteen." He slapped Marie on the butt. "Go help your mother."

"Papa!" squealed Maria as she picked up two bowls from the shelf.

Jean smiled. "It is a pleasure to meet you all. Alain has spoken of you often."

"Come sit." Alain patted one of the two chairs. "Jacqueline, give us a bowl of that excellent stew."

"I already am." She was ladling big scoops of stew into the bowls.

As Marie set them on the table, she looked at Jean. "Oh! You're hurt."

"It's just a cut."

"It needs to be cleaned." She brought over a pitcher of water and a bowl. Using a piece of cloth, she wiped the blood from Jean's face. As she clucked, she said, "It's not bad. Just a cut in the hairline. No one will even notice it."

"Thank you." Jean smiled and watched Marie. She was a plain girl with straight brown hair, but she was healthy. Her hands and face were clean, and the nightgown she wore was mended and well cared for. It was clear her mother and father took good care of her.

Alain leaned into his friend. "I was able to get a pound of fresh meat with my promotion bonus, and we put it all in the stew."

"Promotion?" Jean sat back and stared at Alain. He hadn't noticed it before, but he now saw that Alain had the insignia of a lieutenant on his shoulders. "When did this happen?"

"I received a field promotion last month," beamed Alain. "That's why I'm here. They gave me leave."

"How?"

"Nothing worth remembering," said Alain as his face clouded.

Jean knew not to pursue it. Memories of the battle were best left alone.

"I'm ready to go back with you," pressed Jean.

Alain shook his head. "No. No." That was all he said. He didn't explain. He didn't discuss.

"Please," urged Jean. "The army is where I belong." He waved his arm around the room. "Not some fancy city like Paris."

"I've already arranged for you to work in the hospital."

"But I'm not in the hospital anymore!"

"You're not?"

"No, this morning Napoleon and Jacques-Louis David came to the hospital ward, and I was told to report to David's studio in the Louvre."

Alain grabbed Jean's hand. "That's what you've always dreamed of! Why would you want to go back to the army now?"

Jean looked down and muttered, "I don't belong."

"Nonsense!"

"These people are treacherous. You never know who the enemy is," pleaded Jean. "At least on the battlefield the enemy is always in front of you."

"And you'll probably die on the battlefield, too," replied Alain. "I don't want to argue about this. No matter how bad it is here, it is ten times, no, a thousand times worse in war." A darkness descended over his face as if he were remembering some atrocity.

"It doesn't matter. My father was a soldier." Jean stood. "I was born to be a soldier." He pounded the table. He sat down again. "I'm going back to battle, where I know I'm good. Marengo proved that."

Bang! Alain's fist pounded the table. "I didn't save your life for you to throw it all away."

"But."

"No buts. I promised your father that I would take care of you." He sighed. "I don't want Girard or Alain to follow me. I want them to have a trade. Don't you realize that this is your chance for a real life."

"I don't belong," Jean said stubbornly.

"You don't know that yet. Take the time to find that out."

Jean stared at Alain.

"Please. If not for yourself, then do it for me. If I could change my life, I would."

After a minute, Jean relented. "Okay, I'll go, but if it's wrong, I'm not going back."

Alain slapped Jean on his back. "Remember, they already want you. Otherwise, David would not have picked you."

CHAPTER 9

An Absent Master

In the morning light, Jean walked the length of the Tuileries gardens from the Place de la Concorde to the Louvre along the Seine. He passed a dozen or so statues and continued past the low hedges of the formal gardens. After no sleep and the early morning spent with Alain and his family, Jean wasn't sure why he was heading toward David's studio. Two hours earlier, he would have sworn that this was the last place he would be going to. But here he was walking to the studio.

As he approached the huge U-shaped building, he couldn't figure out where the entrance was. There seemed to be many doors that could possibly lead to the part where the studio was located. The vastness of the palace was disorienting.

Still in uniform himself, he spotted two sentries standing guard. "Excuse me?"

"Yes," answered one of the soldiers.

Jean nodded. "I was wondering how do I get to the studio of Jacques-Louis David?"

The soldier pointed to a small door beside the stables, which led to stairs. The stairs opened on a long hallway lined with incredibly tall windows. Even this early in the morning the corridor was crowded with people going in and out of rooms, talking passionately in groups, or simply eating a brioche or croissant. The people were all dressed well, the men in fashionably cut jackets and trim slacks, the women in finely sewn dresses and wearing elegant hats perched atop their mounded curls. As Jean surveyed the space, he felt shabby in his military uniform. He had not changed or washed since the day before, which wasn't unusual, but the scent of fine perfumes tickling his nostrils made him self-conscious of his own inadequacy.

Jean spotted an open door at the end of the hall. It was the only one on the corridor that was open. Too intimidated to ask anyone for directions, he made for that door first.

Laughter spilled from the room, and Jean poked his head inside. The high-ceilinged room was covered from floor to ceiling with paintings. Large canvases, small canvases, canvases of every size. The floor had beautiful and colorful carpets of different sizes scattered about, some partly on top of each other. Packed almost elbow to elbow were tall easels, at least a dozen. Each easel held a canvas, before which stood an artist holding a brush. Before he could step into the room, two young women pushed him aside and walked into the room giggling. Jean had noticed them in the hallway as they chatted away with another woman. They were both beautiful, but in exactly the same way. They were identical twins, dressed in identical dresses, except one in blue and the other in pink. In this remarkable and extraordinary world that Jean had suddenly stepped into they were not shocking. In fact, these young women were perhaps the only understandable thing in the entire palace. He had seen twins before. He had never seen professional painters.

Jean edged himself against the wall to the right of the door and simply watched. The room was abuzz with chatter as the painters unpacked their brushes and mixed their paints. The sharp smell of kerosene and glue mixed in the air with fabric dust from freshly stretched canvases.

"Maggot!" came a shout above the rumbling of voices.

Jean turned and froze.

"Yes, you!"

Snapping his fingers and pointing directly at him was the belligerent young man who had been Michelle's companion at the café the night before. This morning he was wearing a dirty smock and stood at the front of the room.

Wordlessly, Jean crossed toward the young man. He felt he had made a terrible mistake listening to Alain. He should have insisted on returning with him to the front. As he walked, his fists clenched. At least now he would have the chance to beat this rude piece of donkey droppings senseless. He raised his fist.

"Strip," barked the young man without so much as a glance at Jean.

Jean froze. "What?" he stammered. He didn't understand what this young man meant. "I'm not taking off my clothes."

The young man turned and looked directly at Jean. "I said 'strip.' Our model for the day did not arrive, so you're it." The young man picked up a canvas and set it on an easel. "What are you waiting for?"

Thinking Jules an obnoxious popinjay, Jean wanted to strike him right then and there. He took a step toward Jules. "This should be easy," he muttered under his breath.

Before he could swing, he was interrupted once more. The night before it had been Michelle, this time it was the twins.

"Oh, Jules! Is this the soldier Michelle was telling us about?"

Jules walked away without answering.

"I'm Émilie," said the girl dressed in blue, as she curtsied.

"I'm Pauline," added the other.

Gathering his equilibrium, Jean bowed. "My name is Jean Martin. I've been assigned to Jacques-Louis David's studio to help with a portrait of Napoleon."

"Oh," replied the one named Émilie. "We know that. Papa told us you would be coming this morning." She turned to her sister, and then they both spoke in unison, "That's why we came!" They giggled uncontrollably.

"Émilie! Pauline! Go home!" ordered Jules. Then he looked at Jean. "And you! Take your clothes off."

Things were getting out of control. Jules was acting like he was studio manager, but how could that be? "I'll wait for David." He turned his back on Jules.

"And I am his son," replied Jules impatiently, clapping his hands. "And that means I run his studio. If you're not up there posing by the time he gets here. There will be hell to pay."

Jean tried to process this. What he wanted to do was simply walk out, but something held him back. He knew that if he did, he would never again have a chance like this. This opportunity was all that he had wished for as he slept in cold, wet blankets in the Alps. He decided then that he would make the best of it, at least for now.

He glanced around the studio. No one seemed to be paying attention to Jules and him. He looked at the paintings hung on every available space on the wall. He wanted one of his paintings on that wall, and the only way for that to happen was if he stood his ground. He had learned in the army never to retreat. He would not retreat now.

"But...there are women present," stuttered Jean.

"They have seen it all before."

The girls giggled again.

"Don't worry," said another young man who looked like the younger brother of Jules. He gave Jean a gentle pat on the back for encouragement. "We always work from nude models. We need to get the underlying physical structure of the body before we can lay clothes on top. Otherwise, everything looks stiff and false."

Jean stared at this new person for a moment. He seemed nice, but he could be tricking him. After a moment, he relented. *This was the work I was hired to do*, he reminded himself. *To be Napoleon. Being Napoleon meant that I would sit up there and be drawn and painted by the studio artists.*

Jean nodded and slowly began to unbutton his coat. Though he found the idea of undressing in front of these two girls humiliating, it was his scars that he was most embarrassed about. His skin across his right side and running along his arm and down his leg was chewed up and gnarled from the burns he suffered.

The young man who had spoken to Jean carried a ladder to a platform set at the front of the room. "Ignore Jules," he added. "He's just being his usual obnoxious self."

"Shut up, Eugene."

The young man wiped his hands on his pants and held one out. "I'm Eugene, the middle brother. Jules is older, and the girls are younger." He smiled as he gave a shrug.

With his arm out of one sleeve of his shirt, Jean stopped undressing and shook Eugene's hand. "I'm Jean."

"I know. Michelle told me."

"Michelle knows all of you?" Jean started to look around. "Is she here?"

Eugene shook his head. "She stopped by our house last night."

After Jean finished undressing, Jules commanded, "Sit! When my father arrives, climb the ladder and pose the way we tell you."

Jean nodded and sat, draping his clothes over his lap.

In the back of the room by the door, a roar erupted. Blocked by the easels Jean couldn't see, but he hoped it marked the arrival of David. He stood and wrapped his coat around his shoulders. He was cold and didn't know how he was going to stand or sit in the nude without shivering.

"Girls, it is time to leave," Jean heard David tell his daughters. "We have work to do."

"Good-bye, Jean," called Émilie and Pauline as they left giggling.

Then the man who had plucked him out of the hospital ward emerged from the group of men. He held out his hand. "Jean!" he said energetically. His face erupted into a half smile, with the tumor keeping one side of his face frozen.

"Yes, sire." Jean stood at attention. He couldn't keep his eyes off the deformity on David's face.

"You're no longer in the army, my boy. You don't need to stand at attention." David broke into laughter. "Which of my boys put you up to this?"

"Sir, I don't understand."

"You're only wearing an army coat."

Jean flushed but said nothing. He *did* feel ridiculous.

Jules came up beside his father and whispered in his ear.

"Oh!" David nodded. "Well, let's get on with it."

Jules pointed to the ladder, and Jean began to climb it.

"Without the coat," ordered Jules curtly.

Jean slipped the coat off and climbed to the top of the ladder. "What should I do?" He was half bent in an awkward position to keep his balance.

"That will be good for now."

As the artists in the room began to work, Jean reminded himself that he had experienced a lot worse on the battlefield and in the hospital. Standing nude in a room full of men was nothing new. A soldier's life is not for the modest. "Just let it pass," he muttered. "In time, you will be the one drawing, and someone else will be up here." In the army it was customary for the newest recruit to be assigned the worst duties, like cleaning the latrine. For Jean, this was just one more occasion where he was the new recruit. "It won't always be this way. I just need to wait it out."

"Keep still," ordered Jules.

David moved among the artists, giving praise and advice. At one canvas, he took the student's brush and articulated the sweep of the leg. As David worked with the students, Jules poured his father a cup of coffee with milk and waited on him. Jean observed from atop the ladder how warm their relationship was. Jules seemed like a completely different person than the one he had encountered this morning, as well as the night before. He wasn't angry or confrontational. Instead, he was gentle and solicitous of his father.

The work went on for over an hour. Jean's muscles were aching from standing on the ladder in an awkward position.

Finally, David clapped his hands. "Break!"

"That means you can relax," Eugene said.

Jean slumped against the ladder.

"Would you like something to drink?" Eugene held out a blanket for Jean to wrap himself in.

"Yes." Jean was glad to have the blanket. He was freezing and afraid that he might be getting sick. His entire body ached and his head hurt, but that could be just the result of his hangover and the bruises from his mugging. He needed rest and would get it as soon as he was released from the studio.

Eugene returned with a goblet of wine, and Jean drank deeply.

"Doesn't your father paint?"

Eugene laughed. "Of course he does, but this morning he is instructing. This afternoon he'll begin his drawings of you for the Bonaparte portrait. But first, he likes to watch his students work. It clears his mind and inspires him to do his best work."

Clap! Clap!

The artists resumed their places before their canvases while Jean climbed back up the ladder.

"This time I would like you to sit on the top step and hold your hands out this way." David demonstrated. "As if you were riding a horse."

"Like this?" Jean mirrored David.

"Fine."

The morning progressed like this, with Jean posing for half an hour followed by a short break. At the moment when Jean thought he might pass out from exhaustion, David clapped his hands and they broke for their midday meal.

Émilie and Pauline breezed in, followed by a half dozen servants carrying baskets filled with baguettes, cheese, and wine. The young artists crowded around the women.

"Émilie, will you marry me?"

"Oh, you want my sister, not me," replied Émilie. "She is so much more agreeable."

"No! Marry me, Émilie! You are my true love!"

"But Jean-Auguste, I heard you say the same words to another just yesterday." She laughed coquettishly.

The paint-splattered suitor knelt before her. "Oh, that is a lie! They are all lies. My heart belongs only to you!"

Eugene took Jean by the arm and led him behind a screen next to the platform. "I've taken the liberty of giving you some of my clothes to wear."

"But I have my uniform."

"You won't need it here. In fact, you'll be better off if you don't wear it."

"Why?"

"With my clothes, you won't stand out," said Eugene helpfully. "We're about the same size, so they should fit." Eugene was bigger than his older brother and built much more like Jean.

Understanding that his uniform would garner him no respect here, Jean dressed quickly. The clothes fit well, and he pulled on his own boots. The shirt and pants were made of cotton imported from the Americas. Jean knew this was a real extravagance after years of the British blockade on the newly formed United States.

"Baron!"

Jean heard a shout as he stood buttoning his pants behind the screen. The energy in the studio seemed to suddenly become charged. Jean poked his head around the screen.

"It's so good to see you back," said David as he shook the hand of the well-dressed man.

Jean recognized the baron immediately. It was his mentor Dominique Vivant Denon. The man had changed little since the Egyptian campaign two years earlier. He was a little stouter, but otherwise he was the same.

"The artifacts I collected in Egypt have just arrived," Baron Denon said. A wide smile spread across his face, and his thick eyebrows danced above his eyes. "It is so good to see you, Jacques-Louis. I have missed you so."

"And you, my friend." David embraced the baron.

"Ho!" called the baron when he noticed Jean stepping from behind the screen. "Just the young man I was thinking of." He wound his way through the easels to Jean's side. "I'm so glad to see you here, but how?" He stood, looking amazed at Jean.

"I'm as surprised as you," stammered Jean. "This is my first day."

The baron turned to David. "How did you find this wonderful lad? You must know he has real talent."

"A friend insisted that Father take him in," interrupted Jules. "And from the looks of him, I'd say it was a mistake."

The baron waved Jules off. "Not at all. Not at all. I taught him how to draw on the Egyptian campaign." He beamed at Jean. "He has real talent," he added as he patted Jean on the back.

Jean beamed at the compliment. After a day of being humiliated by Jules, the baron's support was welcome.

"Well, well, well!" David smiled broadly. "Now here is a real surprise. Who would have imagined that you were a protégé of the Baron Dominique Vivant Denon? This is a remarkable turn of events. Just a few hours ago, I was thinking that I was just doing a family friend a favor. Michelle will be pleased to know her good judgment has been confirmed by Baron Denon, no less."

"Michelle Durand made this possible?" Jean blurted out in surprise.

"Why, yes, of course," replied David. Then he turned back to the baron and explained, "The truth be told, I needed someone to sit for the portrait of the First Consul crossing the St. Bernard, which I've been commissioned to do by Charles IV." Charles IV was king of Spain. "Bonaparte refused to sit for the portrait."

"My God! The First Consul has an ego the size of the New World," said the baron.

"At least," laughed David. "But he also has an eye for what really matters. After seeing how much my *Sabines* influenced people, he knows that a painting of him in triumph will win the hearts of all in France." He pulled a newspaper out of his pocket. "See here." He pointed at an engraving of the scene in the hospital. "This happened only yesterday, and he has an illustration of it in the newspaper. Not a day passes without his visage splashed somewhere across Paris."

"He's a genius of propaganda," admitted the baron. "Who will go against him now? If he keeps it up, he'll become emperor of all of Europe."

"But of course! That is his plan," confided David. "He told me himself."

Jean stared awkwardly between the two men. The news of Michelle's intervention came as a surprise, but it pleased him immensely that she had such faith in him. He could barely stand still amongst the two great men and not rush away to find her and thank her.

"Congratulations!" said the baron.

"Thank you! But how can I paint the portrait of someone who is not here?" He pointed to a half-finished portrait of Napoleon hanging on the wall. "I started this in 'ninety-seven, and before I could finish, he ran off on the First Italian Campaign. Now it hangs there as a reminder to me that it will never be done. I still keep it because despite not being finished, it is one of the best portraits I've every done."

Jean was moved by the canvas. The painting showed the head of Napoleon, but his body above the waist was only sketched in and the rest of the canvas was blank.

"Bonaparte wanted me to represent him at the site of one of his victories, at Rivoli, at the foot of the Alps, on horseback, at the head of his staff officers, holding the Treaty of Campo Formio in his hand, anything but a simple portrait." David rubbed his swollen cheek. "I think he tired of this because it *was* just a portrait." He shrugged. "So now I paint the portrait he wants, at the request of King Charles IV of Spain, but he no longer has an interest in sitting even for that."

"Oh, he is not interested in how the portrait looks," laughed Denon. "I traveled to Egypt with him. He could not care less about accuracy. He was only concerned with how the picture would be viewed by the audience. He wants to seduce France, and he knows your painting will make that happen."

"But first, the painting must be art," insisted David. "And without Bonaparte, I am just painting one of my historical paintings."

"Exactly! For Bonaparte, this is what you're painting. You are painting history!"

"I'm not so sure I can do that," said David.

"Tut, tut," clucked the baron. "And what does this boy have to do with this?"

"He's going to be Bonaparte!" said an exasperated David. "I have the First Consul's cape, hat, and sword from the campaign, and I'm to create history out of these trinkets."

"You've spent enough time with Bonaparte to know what he looks like," replied the baron.

David looked pained. "Even my historical paintings had models."

"Well, you have a model," argued the baron. "Besides Jean is much better looking than Bonaparte, and he can keep his face still." The baron was referring to Napoleon's facial tics.

Several of the students laughed.

Jean was surprised to hear the men refer to Napoleon as Bonaparte. In the army, they always called the general by his first name, but here in Paris he was referred to by his last. He didn't understand the difference, but he vowed to remember to do the same.

"Am I right, Jean-Auguste?" asked the baron.

"Most certainly," replied Jean-Auguste-Dominique Ingres, one of David's most promising students.

Several others murmured their ascent.

"It's just that I want to capture the majesty of the moment and of the man...." David trailed off. Despite his friend's confidence in him, David seemed uncertain.

As Jean listened to the exchange, he wondered why his new master would be so concerned. He had heard Napoleon dismiss David's concerns, and now the baron did as well. For Jean, an order by Napoleon would be all that was needed. As a soldier, he was trained never to question a direct order. He didn't understand why David was having so much trouble.

"It just seems impossible to construct a pure composition without the visual center even present," complained David. "But enough of this. Let's eat!" He raised his cup and toasted his friend, the baron.

CHAPTER 10

Class Warfare

"Uh-oh," said Jean the moment he stepped out of the studio into the hall. He tried to duck back into the studio.

"Jean!" Michelle raised her hand to get his attention.

What should I say? What should I say? he repeated to himself in desperation. It had been two days since he had last seen Michelle at the café. Now it was the morning of his second day working in the studio, and here she was. He would have to thank her for all she had done, but he was also angry at her for meddling with his life. He hated that he hadn't done this on his own. As all this ran through his head, Jean tried to calculate whether he could get away, but before he could come up with a plausible excuse, Michelle was standing in front of him.

"Oh, I'm so glad I found you!"

"Me, too." Jean lied.

Michelle's cheeks were flushed, and her smile was breathtaking. Just looking at her made Jean forget about his embarrassment about being so indebted to her. Jean wanted her to like him romantically, but he knew that it wasn't possible. She was with Jules, and he was just a lowly private in the army. Not even in the army anymore. He had no status. He wasn't a soldier, and he wasn't even officially a student in the studio of Jacques-Louis David. He existed in some in-between place. How could he explain to anyone that he was a *sitter pretending to be Napoleon*? He was sitting for a portrait of someone else, not even himself. He didn't rate his own image being reproduced. How could he expect to be attractive to someone so far above his station in life as Michelle?

"Tell me everything!" She grabbed his arm and led him down the hallway and out the door.

"I want to thank you, Michelle," Jean forced himself to tell her. He was really grateful, but at the same time he believed he should have done this on his own. He shouldn't need help from a girl. He was a soldier.

"Let's get something to eat around the corner."

"But I've been sent to bring coffee and breakfast back to the studio," protested Jean.

"Please, Jean," pleaded Michelle. "I'm so sorry about the other night. I wanted you to meet Jules before you went to his father's studio. His family and mine are very close. My father is his father's physician. Jules and I practically grew up together."

The morning sun was low on the horizon, just above the trees that lined the Tuileries. Along the Arc du Carrousel they found the Café de République. A waiter in a crisp white apron led them indoors to a table by the bar.

"Two coffees with milk, please," ordered Jean.

"Oh, and one small roll," added Michelle.

Michelle accidentally brushed Jean's hand with her own. She pulled it back quickly and then blushed. Jean did not know how to respond. He wanted to grab her hand and hold it tight and never let it go, but instead he sat there dumbly. He didn't like being in this position. In the army, there was rarely a moment when he did not know how to act. In the company of Michelle, it seemed as if he had no clue what to say or do around her.

The silence was awkward, but they continued waiting for the order to arrive without saying a word.

"It is not fair," came a shout from the entrance to the café.

Michelle and Jean looked up. Émilie was standing at the door with Pauline behind her. "Michelle! It is not fair that you have this handsome boy all to yourself!" She and her sister bustled into the café and drew up chairs for themselves at the table.

At this moment, Paris seemed to be as small as the tiniest hamlet in the most remote part of France. *Was there anywhere that he could go to find privacy?* Jean wondered.

The waiter arrived immediately to take their orders. The girls each asked for hot chocolate.

As Jean listened to the twins' chatter, he became increasingly annoyed. He wanted to do something to show Michelle that he was worthy of her love. He wanted to earn her respect and adoration. Instead, he sat there mutely as these silly girls chattered on about nothing. If only he could find some way to repay his debt, then she could be grateful to him and the balance of the friendship could swing in his favor.

"Did you hear what Gisette said to Madame Boudreau?"

"No!" gasped Michelle.

Jean had no idea what they were talking about. This was some special world that he was not a part of, so he took a pencil out of his pocket and fished a scrap of paper from another pocket. He began to draw a caricature of the waiter as he stood leaning against the bar chatting with a customer. With a few strokes, the waiter's mustache became twice the size of his head. His ears were made enormous, with hairs protruding. Jean was engrossed and amused by his rendering.

"You!"

Jean recognized the voice and froze.

"You were supposed to bring breakfast an hour ago!"

Jean looked up at Jules with murderous eyes. He knew if it came to it he could kill Jules, but he wasn't about to lose his composure in front of Michelle one more time. He tried to explain, "I was asked out to…"

"I don't care if Bonaparte himself asked you to breakfast. Your job is to get breakfast for the studio."

Jean and Jules glared at each other.

"It's my fault," interrupted Michelle.

"And ours," added Pauline.

"I insisted that Jean take me out for coffee," said Michelle. "Jules, don't be such a bore."

"Go, maggot!"

Michelle put her hand on Jean's arm. "You better go, Jean."

Jean got up, but he stood and stared at Jules full in the face before brushing by him to leave. "I'll go because I want to, not because I was told to."

Jules took his seat. "Don't forget the croissants!" He added.

"Stop being so rude!" Jean heard Michelle admonish Jules as he left the café. Down the street was a bakery, where he bought a dozen croissants and a dozen brioches. On the next block, a street vendor sold buckets of hot coffee with milk. Jules purchased one. On his way back to the studio, he found Michelle waiting for him in the courtyard.

"I really do want to hear about everything," she said.

"Don't patronize me," Jean replied curtly. He pushed his way into the building, annoyed that he could ever think that he could join her world. He would always be an outsider. He would always be the errand boy. At least he would have art, and that was worth the small indignities that he would have to suffer.

CHAPTER 11

A Family Alone

Perched on the edge of a worn bench in the studio, Jean stirred a pot of glue heating in the fireplace. He moved a long wooden spoon around in a mixture of powdered rabbit-skin glue, an equal quantity of water, a tablespoon of white vinegar, and a pungent drop of purified ox bile. He had been given this recipe from David himself. To Jean's regret, Jules had overseen the preparation of materials with a careful attention to detail. Jean had spent six hours cooking this mixture until the ingredients were fully absorbed, and now it was nearly done. Along the wall, canvases, which were stretched with tightly woven linen with threads of warp and woof in equal weight and strength, were stacked.

Jules looked over his shoulder. "The glue is ready."

Jean lifted the pot from the fire and set it on the floor by the canvases.

"Don't spill any," barked Jules.

Of course that made Jean spill the glue.

"You idiot! Clean it up."

Jean grabbed a rag and wiped the floor. The glue smeared, making a larger area sticky.

"Let me do this," said Jules impatiently. He dipped the rag in turpentine and then wiped up the glue. "You have no talent for the craft."

"Jules!" said David firmly from across the studio. "That's enough. Go home."

"Yes, Papa." Jules gathered his things and left quickly.

Now only Jean and David remained in the studio. Jean had hoped for a moment like this, being left alone with the master.

David dipped a wide brush into the glue and spread it across the canvas. "It is essential that the paint never comes into direct contact with the linen, or the fabric will rot." He spread more glue across the canvas. "This is the way it's been done for hundreds of years. It's called sizing the canvas."

Jean nodded.

"You try it."

Jean took the brush and dipped it into the pot. He spread the glue evenly across the canvas.

"Good, good." David watched him finish the canvas and begin on another. There were ten that needed to be sized.

"When do we mix the colors?"

"Tomorrow, Jules will go to the colorman and place the order."

Jean swallowed hard. The last thing he wanted to do was spend more time with Jules, but at the same time he was desperate to learn more about making colors. "Can I go and help him?" Jean thought that perhaps when they were alone he could make friends with Jules. He knew that if he didn't, Jules had the power to make his life miserable.

David seemed to hesitate, but then said, "Good, I think Jules will not be happy, but you two must learn to work together if you're going to remain."

"Thank you."

"Make sure you do them all tonight. I am going now." The great painter took off his smock and hung it on a peg. He shrugged into his coat.

Long after the dinner hour, Jean made his way through the dimly lit streets to Alain's apartment. After two days at the studio, he had so much he wanted to share. He felt he would simply burst with the news if he didn't tell Alain.

Jean almost leaped in one bound up the rickety stairs to the second-floor landing. He pounded his fist on the door with excitement.

Silence.

He knocked again.

After a moment, he could hear movement inside. Finally, a sleepy voice asked through the door, "Who's there?"

"It's me! Jean!"

The lock on the door turned, and the door swung open. "Jean!" Marie stood sleepy-eyed at the door.

"Oh!" In his excitement, Jean had forgotten the time. "I didn't realize it was so late. I was preparing canvases and…"

"Come in," insisted Marie.

"Don't worry. You are always welcome here," said Jacqueline as she crossed the room.

"Jean!" cried the boys as they jumped out of bed and ran to him.

"Papa is gone," said little Alain.

"He was called back to his regiment," explained Marie.

Jacqueline grabbed Jean's arm. "Come in and eat something. We have bread and cheese."

Jean sat at the table while the family stood around him.

"Well?" inquired Marie.

"Well, what?"

"How'd it go?"

"Oh, it is wonderful," replied Jean. "The first day was horrible. They made me pose for hours in very uncomfortable positions." Jean laughed. "My muscles hurt so much that I couldn't move."

"And today?"

"Well, today started out just as bad," said Jean. "Jules, David's son, has it in for me, but David spent so much time with me and showed me how to prepare canvases." He paused and looked at Alain's family. For a moment, he had a pang of jealousy. He wished he had a family, too. "I learned so much. And tomorrow I'm going to see how paint is made!"

Jacqueline set the bread and cheese on the table. "I'm sorry, but we only have water."

Jean tore a piece of the bread. It was stale and hard. The cheese was covered in mold and looked as if it had been fished out of the garbage. He took a bite of each to be polite, but it was clear to him that they did not have much food. He looked at the shelf above the stove and saw that it was empty. This bread and cheese was the last that they had.

"Do you want some?" he asked the boys.

They greedily swallowed the food.

"When did Alain leave?"

"Right after you," said Jacqueline. "A messenger came with an order that he report to his regiment immediately."

"I so wanted to tell him everything," blurted Jean.

"I know he wanted to hear, but…" Jacqueline's voice trailed off.

"I should be with him," said Jean.

"Don't be foolish, Jean," said Jacqueline quickly. "Alain is a soldier through and through. You're just at the start of your journey."

Jean stared at the table, unable to look at anyone.

"Alain would be disappointed if you didn't take this chance," she added.

"But it feels like the coward's way out," admitted Jean.

"You've proven your courage on the battlefield," she answered emphatically. "Now is your chance to use that courage and succeed where Alain and any of us could never."

Jean sighed. "I know you're right. You've said nothing that I haven't thought myself, but I don't like abandoning friends."

"You're not," said Marie. "Alain spoke of nothing else but your talent as an artist. I've already said this, but I'll say it again and again until you accept it: Alain would be disappointed if you did not pursue it."

Jean felt awkward being put on the spot. He tried to laugh it off and pulled a sheet of paper and a pencil from his pocket. "Then I better get at it." He turned to the boys and asked, "Who should I draw first?"

"Me!" shouted Girard.

"No, me!" chimed little Alain.

"Well, I can't decide, so I'll draw you both together."

With only a stub of candle left, the light in the apartment was dim, but for Jean these boys shone with a light brighter than a hundred candles. He quickly sketched the shapes of their faces and the shape of their bodies in their bedclothes. As he stared intently at the two boys, he noticed how thin they were. Their eyes bulged above their hollow cheeks. Their collarbones jutted sharply out of their shirts.

"Did Alain leave you with money to get by?" Though it was rude to ask, he had to know.

"We'll get by. I take in laundry."

Jean noticed the large pot on the stove and the clothes hanging to dry. Jacqueline and Marie had not been asleep, as he had assumed. They were up late washing clothes. A heavy iron warmed on the stove to press the wrinkles out of the clothes.

Jean dug the few coins he had out of his pocket and set them on the table. "I don't need this. They feed me at the studio, and I sleep on a mat in the corner."

"We can't take your money, Jean," protested Jacqueline.

"I hate having money," insisted Jean. "I never know what to do with it."

"What about fun? Don't you want to enjoy yourself?"

"I'm already enjoying myself. Just being in David's studio is the dream of my life." He picked up his pencil. "Now stop interrupting me or I'll never finish."

"Yeah, we want our picture," shouted the boys.

Jacqueline held up her hands. "I know when to admit defeat."

Jean quickly finished the drawing and signed his name with a flourish. Girard snatched it away from the table.

"It looks like me!" shouted Girard.

His mother wrapped her arms around Girard. "I'll take that. I don't want it to be ruined."

"Perhaps someday, I can do a real portrait."

"This is beautiful, Jean."

"I just wish I could give you something you need instead of a simple drawing," said Jean as he got ready to leave.

CHAPTER 12

Drawing a Lesson

"This is azure." The colorman pointed to a chart with dozens of dabs of oil paints labeled under each color.

"The blue is very rich." Jean replied as he rubbed his finger over the dried paint. He had never really worked with paint. In Egypt, he had watched some of the painters work, but Jean was never able to get close because he was assigned to assist Denon, who was an engraver. Thus, Jean knew well the engraver's tools, the pen and ink, the acids, the wax, the copper plates.

"Yes, it's made from the finest lapis lazuli mined in Afghanistan." Behind the colorman, shelves were lined with dozens of jars filled with pigments. Against another wall were barrels of linseed oil and other mediums in which to suspend the pigments.

"What market?" asked Jules.

"Venice, of course." The colorman was old and had a long, gray beard. He had clearly made the trip to Venice for the famed ultramarine many times. No other market carried the Afghani azure. Tucked away in the most remote valleys and mountains, the lapis lazuli mines were some of the most closely held secrets in the world. Few traders made the long journey to the East, and even fewer returned. Between the rough landscape and the thieves, the road to these mines was treacherous.

As Jean leaned in to see the color chart more clearly, his head ached. Earlier, he had made it back to the studio in time to get a few hours sleep, but it was not enough. After breakfast, he joined Jules on this errand to the colorman's shop where oil paints were manufactured. It had only been in the past few decades that artists had stopped mixing paint themselves. David believed Viggo Aurelia's workshop to be the best in Paris because Viggo was old enough to have learned the old ways from the masters. Viggo used ancient recipes, which made his colors richer and purer. The old man didn't take short cuts or use inferior substitutes when he did not have the very best ingredients on hand.

The three men sat at a table by the store's window. Sunlight streamed in, giving the page of samples luminescence.

"What is this green called?" Jean rubbed the tip of his finger over a rich green. It was so deeply hued, it almost seemed to have a texture all its own, even though the sample was flat.

"*Terre vert*. Green earth. It comes from another ground mineral."

"What mineral?" asked Jean. This was all very interesting. Color had always seemed a mystery to him. He had always assumed that they were simply made, but now he was learning that they came from different minerals and plants.

"That's a secret," laughed Viggo. "But I can show you how we make paint." He went to one of the shelves and took down a glass jar filled with a finely ground pigment the color of yellow. He poured a very small quantity on a marble-topped counter. "This yellow is called gamboge. It comes from the gum resin of an evergreen that grows in southeast Asia. The resin is gathered after it oozes out of cuts made in the bark of the tree."

"Have you ever seen these trees?" asked Jean.

"Oh, of course! I have been to the Far East many times," said Viggo. "By boat and by land." He picked up a palette knife and made a well in the small portion of powder. "The resin is dried and then ground into a powder to be mixed with the oil."

He reached under the counter and took out a vessel.

"Linseed oil." He poured less than a spoonful in the crater. "Now I turn the pigment into the oil." He carefully used his palette knife to mix the pigment with the oil. "As you do this, you press down with your palette knife and blend until you have a smooth paste." He worked the oil and pigment for several minutes. "You need a strong palette knife for this." He pressed the knife down on the marble until it bent dramatically. "Otherwise, the knife will break."

"The color is beginning to glow," observed Jean.

"Yes, and it's done." Viggo smiled.

"That was easy," said Jean.

"Not when you're making large quantities and storing them in tubes," said Viggo. "That's where problems occur. The pigment needs to be stable for days, not just hours. If you suspend the pigment properly in the linseed oil, it will make the most marvelous colors."

Jean smiled.

"Colors that remind us that the Lord is always present," added Viggo.

"Good, Viggo, enough with the lesson," interrupted Jules. "We need to get back to the studio. We'll take the azure, terre vert, and burnt umber, and suspend them all in sun-thickened linseed oil."

"Ah, you want the paint to have texture." The colorman calculated the cost, and Jules paid him. "Tell your father I'll have the paints to you tomorrow."

Jules and Jean left the shop to return to the studio.

"How long have you run your father's studio," asked Jean as they rode in a carriage through the city.

"This is my first year," replied Jules.

"Do you paint as well? I haven't seen you working in the studio."

"I haven't had time," he replied curtly. "Running the studio and making sure novices like you are on time and prepared takes every minute of the day." After a few moments, he shifted his gaze forward again.

Jean remained silent through the rest of the ride as well. He wondered if perhaps Jules's animosity was really just hazing. He remembered the many humiliations he had to suffer when he first joined the army. Other soldiers constantly picked on him until he proved that he belonged. Over time, he will prove himself and then be accepted by Jules.

"This might not be as difficult as counting how many angels can dance on the head of a pin, but still…" sighed David. He stood in front of his drawing and marked an X across the center of the paper.

Wearing Napoleon's bicorn hat, riding boots, and cloak from Marengo, Jean sat straddling a stepladder. He felt silly sitting up there.

"Move your knees higher," asked the young student named Ingres.

Jean complied. He so wanted to be down there drawing instead of playing Napoleon.

"Lift the sword," said Jules. He demonstrated by holding his arm up. "Point toward the sky with it."

Jean waved the ornate Mameluke sword. "You know this isn't the sword Bonaparte carries into battle."

"We're making a painting, not going into battle," sniped Jules as his hand moved quickly across the paper, trying to capture the energy and movement that Jean's pose embodied. "And, Jean…notice my hand on the brush." He shot Jean a withering look of contempt.

Jean smiled back sweetly while thinking what a bastard Jules was.

"This is a disaster," moaned David, not noticing the tension between Jules and Jean. "I'm just not inspired."

"But your historical paintings are so beautifully imagined," protested Jean from atop his perch.

"That's the problem," said David as he sat before his easel. "I could choose the drama in a historical painting. All I see here is Bonaparte sitting on a horse."

Despite himself, Jean began to laugh.

"Hold still," said Jules. "I'm trying to get the sword right."

"What's so funny?" asked David irritably.

"Well, there wasn't anything dramatic about Napoleon crossing the St. Bernard Pass," said Jean. He took the bicorn hat off and held it in his lap. "The First Consul rode a mule over the pass. It was cold, and we had to move quickly in order to surprise the Austrians, so it felt like we were running up the mountain. We didn't really rest until we made the monastery. And then only for four hours."

"So I should paint our First Consul on a slow mule with soldiers running a foot race around him?" laughed David. "That would make Bonaparte happy. No wonder he wants me to *imagine* the scene. Historical accuracy doesn't serve his purpose—and I suppose it doesn't serve mine either."

"You could paint all the soldiers running in the nude," added Jules.

Jean looked down at Jules. He was surprised he had a sense of humor. "Actually, we were all covered in mud."

David smiled. "That would certainly cause more trouble than my *Sabine Women*."

"Napoleon could be dressed like the Sabine women while his soldiers could wearing nothing," smirked Ingres. "I wonder what that allegory would be?"

"Allegory?" asked Jean, not knowing what the word meant.

"Yes," said David as he looked up to Jean. "Every painting represents something more than just the image that is depicted."

"Take the *Sabine Women*," added Ingres. "Set in the early days of Roman history, the Romans have abducted the daughters of their neighbors, the Sabines."

"I know," said Jean defensively. He was self-conscious about never going to school. He didn't want it known just how uneducated he was.

"To avenge this kidnapping, the Sabines attack," continued Ingres. "But a problem has arisen. Hersilia, the daughter of the Sabine leader Tatius has since married Romulus, the Roman leader, and has had two children with him."

"Ah, women," interrupted Jules. "They are the source of all our trouble."

The men laughed.

"But that's not the point, Jules," said Ingres as he sat at the edge of the platform underneath Jean. "Jacques-Louis's painting captures that moment of supreme tension when Hersilia steps in between the two sides and exhorts the warriors not to take wives from husbands and mothers from children."

Jean was reminded of Michelle standing between Jules and him that night at the café, but for the life of him he could not come up with any allegorical meaning. To Jean, Jules was a selfish idiot and nothing more. There didn't need to be any more meaning than that.

"This was one of those great moments in history," explained David with passion, "that could reveal so much about ourselves."

"A heroic moment," added Ingres.

The studio became silent. Finally, Jean couldn't stand it anymore. "So what's the allegory in the *Sabine Women*?"

David raised his eyebrows. "Perhaps we'll never know…"

Ingres and Jules laughed.

Jean knit his brow. He thought perhaps they were teasing him. *Could it be that David's* The Intervention of the Sabine Women *was an allegory against war?*

Jules took over. "What we need is to focus on the composition."

Nods all around. At this stage of the creation of a painting, this is what a studio was for. Discussing, conceptualizing, sketching, pulling together all the ideas for a composition. David instructed his students how this was done, at the same time soliciting ideas.

"What do we know the painting must include?"

"That you've been paid a commission of twenty-four thousand francs by Charles IV," joked Ingres.

"Bonaparte," said Jean, getting back to the discussion.

"Yes, but also his mount," said Georges, another student of David's.

"And the mountain," said Ingres. "It has to look like Bonaparte has conquered the Alps."

"Perfect," said David. "It has to be Napoleon, but ten times so! Napoleon is France, and the French Republic is at the pinnacle of civilization. We must show the world why France's destiny is to rule the world with liberty and fraternity."

Jean began to climb down the ladder. His rear end was sore from straddling a thin plank of wood, and it was clear they were going to be talking this out for a while instead of drawing.

"Jean-Auguste, you go work on getting Bonaparte's features," said Jules.

"Yes, I want to capture his sense of destiny, so I'll need you to watch him carefully," added David, "and take Jean with you as an assistant. You'll need one."

Jean nodded, but he wasn't paying attention.

"What's wrong?" asked David.

"I have a splinter." He pulled at the seat of his pants until he extricated the sliver of wood. "But that sounds wonderful. Can I draw as well?"

"Absolutely!" replied David. "The baron says you have a real talent."

"Well, wait until you see before you offer any praise," said Jean.

Jules ignored this exchange and continued the assignments.

"Georges, you will focus on the landscape. We'll need to get many sketches of the mountains."

"Very well."

"Pierre and Etienne, you'll need to spend time with the artillery and infantry—make sure you get their uniforms correct."

"I'll want Bonaparte in the foreground, but the army needs to be included and clearly under his control," explained David. "How we will resolve that, I don't know."

"If Bonaparte is in the foreground, then the soldiers and their equipment will be smaller," said Jean demonstrating that he understood perspective. "Perhaps the First Consul should tower over the army."

"He should be on one of the peaks of the Alps," said David. "Good, Jean!"

Jean stood straighter after the praise.

"Finally, I must take the problem of the horse," continued David. "I don't know how we'll make the horse look realistic. I want the horse to be rearing, but I'll have to imagine it since I can't get a horse to stand on its hind legs while I draw it."

The men put away their drawing materials.

"Let's get a bite to eat at the café and call it a day," said David.

CHAPTER 13

Everybody Loves
a Parade

The cheers could be heard blocks away. Jean and Ingres climbed into the carriage that would take them to Versailles. Just outside of Paris, the palace had been the seat of government and capital of the kingdom of France until Louis XVI was returned to Paris in 1789 and then executed in 1792.

"I don't know why he's out there," said Ingres as he sat down on the blue velvet seat inside the cab. "It's completely empty since the revolutionary council sold off much of the palace's contents."

"Why did they do that?"

"To raise money, I guess. But I also think they wanted to get rid of everything that reminded the country of the kings of France."

The carriage clattered down the street.

"All the art went to the Louvre for the people's museum. The medals and books went to the National Library, and all the clocks and scientific instruments were collected in the newly formed School of

Arts and Letters." Ingres turned toward Jean. "Did you know that Louis XVI loved clocks. He collected all kinds of them. Spent millions of francs on them."

"While the people starved in the streets," added Jean.

"Don't believe everything you hear," said Ingres. "Especially that."

Just then, a roar from a crowd drifted toward the carriage.

"What is that sound?" asked Jean. He glanced out the window but only saw a few pedestrians and carriages.

Ingres rapped on the roof of the carriage. "Take us to the parade."

The carriage turned down a side street.

"There's one of these almost every day now," said Ingres. "It's the only way to keep our fellow citizens behind the regime. They wave sabers and march in unison, and the people get excited."

"Well, you need the people behind the army," replied Jean testily. He was annoyed by Ingres's apparent cynicism. "My friends are dying for these people. It's important for them to be reminded of that."

The carriage drew up to the end of the block.

"Come," said Ingres. He exited the carriage and pushed through the crowded sidewalk.

Row after row of soldiers marched in step down the broad avenue. In their parade dress uniforms, the soldiers made a spectacular display.

"They look magnificent!" exclaimed Jean. He wished that he was still in uniform and not in the clothes that Eugene had given him. "Do you know where they're returning from?"

Ingres laughed. "Returning from? Why the suburbs of Paris." He waved his hand airily toward the regiment. "They're the Paris guard. They march through the city twice a week because Bonaparte knows that the people love a spectacle."

"It's good that they train so regularly. In my regiment, when we weren't on the march, we drilled and drilled," said Jean. "We had to learn to trust one another. The best way when not in battle was to march and march, seemingly linked by our heartbeats. It was the only way we could work together as one being."

Ingres studied Jean as he spoke. "I know you're right," he replied slowly. "And I have to admit that with so many countries trying to threaten us because they perceive us as a weak and vulnerable new country, we have to be strong and ready." He paused and watched the soldiers pass. "But at the same time, I can't help but hear Bonaparte's cynicism echo through my head."

"Cynicism? What do you mean?"

Ingres turned to his young friend and looked sad. "The last time I accompanied Bonaparte and Jacques-Louis on one of their morning walks, the First Consul said something about giving the people a good parade and they will follow you anywhere."

"No, I'm sure he didn't mean it that way," replied Jean. "He's a great general and knows how to gain the support of the people. I saw it on the battlefield. I would have followed him anywhere after he visited the victims of the plague in Jerusalem. To put his own life in jeopardy just to support the suffering proved how much he cares."

"He visited plague victims?" asked Ingres, surprised.

"Yes, the entire Egyptian campaign was a disaster, but the worst of it was that we lost more to the plague than we ever did to the enemy, and Bonaparte made sure that the sick were taken care of." Jean remembered Napoleon ignoring his guard and entering the Mohamed Ali mosque, which the army was using as a temporary hospital for plague victims. While his officers stood in the street afraid to enter, Napoleon went from bed to bed and spoke with each and every victim. No one would follow into these wards. When he finally emerged and did not come down with the plague, Napoleon's reputation as an immortal only increased. The army would suffer any trial to follow him.

The two watched the parade in silence.

"I would not be here if he didn't care for his men," pressed Jean. "I would have died at Marengo."

"Come," said Ingres gently. "We have to return to the carriage. We have work to do."

"You don't understand," pressed Jean.

"Understand what?"

"A soldier has to know in his heart that his general would sacrifice his own life for the soldier's safety. Otherwise, the soldier will never throw himself into the insanity of battle. Napoleon proved that to us. These parades." He motioned back to the boulevard where the soldiers marched. "The people need to know this. And if these spectacles do that, then good."

Ingres smirked. "Perhaps." As the two men returned to the waiting carriage, he added, "Judge for yourself this afternoon."

Ingres's smugness irritated Jean, but he held his tongue.

CHAPTER 14

Farewell to Egypt

"I packed an easel for you," said Ingres as they passed through the gates of the Palace of Versailles. "Jacques-Louis planned on you assisting me, but Bonaparte would ask why you weren't drawing as well since you are from the studio. Then he would become difficult because he would believe that we didn't respect him enough to send two artists."

"Thanks," said Jean. "I can draw. I learned from the baron."

"I heard, but I haven't seen what you can do, and the baron...well, let's just say he'll exaggerate a little when it suits him."

To be sketching the great Napoleon, the man he had followed into battle, was beyond a dream. It was like he had suddenly arrived in paradise. Jean tried to imagine what the Palace of Versailles would look like. He had seen the great mosques of the Middle East with their grand minarets and exotic tile work, and he had heard that Versailles was at least as grand, but in a completely different way. The baron had even compared Versailles to the mosques, claiming the mosques were clearly inferior.

"I'm just going to have to trust that you can draw," said Ingres. He sat back and exhaled tensely. "This could go either really well or disastrously."

"Why?" asked Jean.

"Jacques-Louis needs Bonaparte's payment for an earlier work. I am to collect it while I'm there." Ingres pulled on his jacket collar nervously. "If we displease him, we surely won't get the money."

The carriage pulled up to the palace entrance.

As the two exited, Jean said, "If Versailles is empty, why does Nap...Bonaparte come here?" Jean gaped at the grand scale of the palace, but was surprised at how decrepit it was. The courtyard was filled with artillery and horses. The beautiful gardens that the baron had described in such detail were an overgrown and tangled shadow of his descriptions. They were so neglected that it looked as if it would be better to simply burn them to the dirt.

Ingres shrugged. "Perhaps he likes the solitude." Jean was impressed with Ingres's ease and comfort in this strange and wonderful new world. He vowed to watch the man closely and follow his lead whenever possible.

They passed the occasional guard as they carried their materials through the long hallways in the palace. Each room they passed through had grand twenty-foot ceilings and polished marble floors, but were stripped bare of furniture and curtains. An occasional window was broken, and the cool outside air rushed in.

"Where are we going?"

"The Hall of Mirrors." Ingres shifted the easel from one hand to the other. "I think Bonaparte likes to look at himself." As Ingres made this remark, they approached a pair of tall, gold-embossed doors. The palace felt like an ornately decorated tomb. As Jean realized this, he remembered that it was a sepulcher for an ancient and soon-forgotten regime, the kings of France.

Two guards stood at attention at the doors. "Do you have business with the First Consul?" asked one rather stiffly. Neither guard actually looked at them. Their eyes were focused directly in front of them, into the middle distance.

"We're from Jacques-Louis David's studio," explained Ingres. "We're here to draw the First Consul." He set down the equipment he was carrying and pulled out a piece of paper.

The guard knocked on the door. It swung open, and he entered. The door closed behind him. A moment later he returned. "This way."

Jean and Ingres entered the long hall. To their right, tall windows lined the entire length, about seventy-five yards. On their left the hall was lined with gilt-trimmed mirrors. Jean had never seen such a magnificent room. It was larger than anything he had seen in the Louvre, which until then was the most impressive place he had ever seen. The only thing that could compare was a cathedral, but they were built in honor of God, so they had to be large. They had to remind everyone of the kingdom of Heaven on earth. This room, the Hall of Mirrors, was a tribute to the royal family. Perhaps God felt that such a place was blasphemy, and that is why they were overturned.

To take this thought to its furthest conclusion, Jean wondered if the next occupier of this hall would experience a similar fate. Before he could consider this fully, they were crossing the hall toward the First Consul.

Despite the grandeur, the room was strangely empty except for a large desk, at which sat Napoleon. He sat sideways in a gilt chair and signed his name quickly on one document after another as several government ministers stood around him. There were no other chairs in the room, so everyone had to stand.

As their footsteps echoed loudly through the hall, Napoleon paused from his work and watched them. "Oh, good! You're here." He stood

and met them in the middle of the hall. Their reflections repeated themselves up and down the room. "Have you been to Versailles before?"

"No," replied Jean.

"Well, this is the Hall of Mirrors. It was constructed in 1678, soon
after the signing of the Treaty of Nijmegen. Louis XIV asked Le
Brun to depict himself in different poses in the ceiling of the
chamber." Napoleon pointed. "Here, he is shown as a Roman
emperor; there, as the leader of France; and over here, as a victorious
war chief." Napoleon seemed to be as impressed with his surround-
ings as was Jean.

"The murals are extraordinary."

"Yes, they do ennoble the poor bastard. But no more. The
Bourbons have been relegated to the dunghill of history," said
Napoleon rather winsomely. "History is always told by the victor."
He returned to his desk. "And that is why you are here. We must tell
the story of the greatness of the French Republic."

Jean smiled. It was inspiring to be in the general's presence. He
opened the portable easel and tightened the bolts. He balanced a sketch
pad on it and opened the pencil and charcoal case. If he never drew
another day, it would be all right with Jean. He was in Versailles
drawing Napoleon from life.

He was so nervous that his hands shook. He could barely hold on
to his pencil.

Napoleon smiled. "Just do your job, soldier."

Jean stood at attention. Suddenly, he relaxed. Being spoken to as a
soldier had a calming effect on him. His hand stilled, and he began to
make marks on the page. Beside him Ingres was doing the same, but he
seemed much more at ease.

As they worked, a messenger arrived with a briefcase. Napoleon
opened the case and read the note. He turned to one of his ministers.

"Egypt is ready to fall. The British have control of the Mediterranean. Their ships are off the coast of Alexandria right now, ready to make land."

A tall thin man with a long mustache and a straight back spoke first. "We will have to abandon our troops."

Napoleon considered the advice. He stood and paced the length of the room. "I think you're right, Georges."

"How many troops are you planning on leaving to the British?" asked another minister, who was short and squat, the physical opposite of the first minister.

"At least twenty thousand," replied the first minister.

"We can't do it," said the squat minister. "What kind of message would this send to the Reserve Army? That we let our troops fall into enemy hands without a fight?"

"It would be a slaughter anyway," said Napoleon. "We've barely been holding onto Alexandria ever since last year. The only other option is to invade the Middle East again." He pulled a piece of paper from the table, crumpled it, and threw it against one of the windows.

Jean listened with alarm. All he could think about was how the army had battled in the blistering heat for nothing. He couldn't believe that Napoleon would just leave twenty thousand men to be executed in cold blood by the hated British.

"I advise, your Excellency, that we find a way to negotiate with the English for a withdrawal," said the squat minister.

"It's a waste of time," argued the tall minister. "Let the British have that godforsaken hell."

"I agree with you, François," replied Napoleon. "If only it were that simple, I'd leave the troops to the British."

Jean wanted to say something, but he felt Ingres's hand on his arm. He glanced at his friend, who quietly pleaded with him to say nothing. Jean nodded. Ingres was right. This was neither the time nor the place to suggest policy to the First Consul. In truth, there was never a good time or place to do something like that. He was simply the sitter for Napoleon's portrait. That he had advanced this far in so little time and was now drawing the famous general was beyond logic. To challenge his luck any further would have been extreme folly.

Jean focused his attention on the receding line of Napoleon's jaw. It was the only part of the general's face that seemed immobile, so Jean used it as a visual anchor upon which to build the portrait. Napoleon was such a bundle of facial tics that otherwise Jean could not hold the man in his gaze.

Napoleon sighed. "I hate to say this, but we're going to have to negotiate with the English." He then took out a fresh piece of paper and wrote something. "Tell them we'll let them have all of Egypt if they allow free passage for our troops." He slipped the message into the briefcase and handed it to the messenger.

The messenger left.

While Jean worked, willing himself to forget what he had just heard, he felt himself shifting. Thinking as a soldier, he could only care about the soldiers who surrendered or died, the battles lost. But studying the First Consul's face, he focused on visual concerns, something he could control with his own hands. He knew he couldn't save the battle over Egypt, and now he knew Napoleon couldn't either. This realization made the face before him, despite the constant twitching, all the more human.

After a while, Napoleon stood and looked over the artists' shoulders. "Hmmm."

Jean felt self-conscious and stopped working. He looked at the general, who was no taller than Jean when he was sitting on a stool.

"Make sure you capture the sense of urgency and destiny. No one will follow me if they do not believe fate has led me here," Napoleon said. "Truth is not half so important as what people think to be true. A painting can shape people's beliefs in a way that no words possibly ever can. It can stir the heart, where words stir the mind. But it is the heart that leads men to sacrifice."

Jean was moved by the First Consul's words. He would love to be able to move hearts and souls with a painting. He believed that only the most noble of causes could be elevated by art and hoped that he would some day learn to do this himself.

Napoleon began to pace the hall as if he were tiring of the palace. The repetition of his reflection followed him throughout the hall as if he were many times the same person. Jean was mesmerized by the reflections. In one instant, he could see all sides of the First Consul. He wondered if it were ever possible to truly see someone completely, both the good and the bad. It made him wonder if *anyone* was all good or all bad.

Snap! His stick of charcoal snapped, and it was as if a magical spell had also been broken. Napoleon returned to his desk and began gathering his papers.

"We need to go," he said.

Ingres immediately began packing their materials. Jean placed the sketch pads in a carrying case and broke down the easels.

Napoleon and his retinue were the first to leave. Jean noticed that they marched behind Napoleon with a deference usually reserved for a king.

As they disappeared out of sight, Ingres visibly relaxed. Then he stiffened. "Damn!"

"What?" asked Jean. He was feeling that this was truly a magical day, even better than the day before, which he thought would never be surpassed.

"I forgot to get the payment," groaned Ingres. "Jacques-Louis will kill me." He slammed the drawing case shut. "That man turns me upside down when I am with him." He started to walk out of the gallery. Jean followed. "No one else does it to me. Even when I was a boy, Jacques-Louis couldn't fluster me like Bonaparte."

"There is an aura that makes him seem better than other men," said Jean. "In the army, men would lay down their lives when Napoleon asked. I'm talking about selfish men. Men who would rob a blind beggar if they had the opportunity."

"You are right, my friend."

A few minutes later, riding in the carriage on their way back to Paris, Ingres spoke, "Well, show me what you did."

Nervously, Jean pulled out his sketch pad and opened it to the pages with that day's drawings. He was certain Ingres would laugh when he saw how amateurish his lines were. His would never compare to the young students in David's studio.

Ingres studied Jean's work in silence. He would look at one page and turn to another, and then return to the first. He examined the drawings so closely, he seemed to be memorizing each line.

Trying to give Ingres privacy, Jean watched the countryside pass by the window. He saw how the fields were replaced by scattered houses and shacks, which in turn were replaced by wooden buildings, and finally those of stone and brick. By the time they reached the Louvre, Jean thought he was going to explode if Ingres did not say anything.

Finally, Ingres closed the sketch pad and said, "These are good. Really good."

CHAPTER 15

Dinner and a Drawing

Jean clutched the note in his hand as he dashed from the Louvre. He headed straight for the Café Violin. This early in the evening the restaurant was bustling with activity. Several men sat out front smoking pipes and cigars. Jean wrinkled his nose at the smell of the burning tobacco. Tobacco was still a new experience for him. In Paris, it was quite popular but expensive. He had shared a pipe once in Egypt. The black leaf burned his throat and made him lightheaded. He figured if he was going to get what he called "drifty," he would rather do it with cognac or wine, which could be had just about anywhere and at little cost.

In fact, military life had given him a taste for drink. As part of his provisions, he was allocated one quart of cognac every day. He had found it impossible to drink that much in a day without being completely incapable of functioning. Alain had told him that a drunk army was a happy army, but that he should stay away from it if he wanted to stay alive. Though Alain drank prodigiously, he was never drunk on duty. In fact, he usually abstained if battle was imminent. Jean had followed his lead at first, but found that even a small amount of cognac made him unable to function properly, so he sold his allotment each day and pocketed the extra money. The only time he did drink while in the military was to celebrate or when the water was too foul to drink.

As Jean pushed through the doors of the café, his eyes darted around the small room in search of Michelle. He didn't know what time it was, and he was afraid that he had missed her. When he saw that she wasn't there, he found a seat and ordered.

As the waiter returned with his sandwich, Michelle breezed through the doors. She waved.

"I got your note," said Jean as Michelle sat at the café table. He held up the crumpled piece of paper and smiled.

"Well, that make sense since here you are," she laughed lightly. She seemed in extraordinarily good spirits. Her cheeks had a reddish hue to them. Her blue eyes seemed to sparkle. Her hair was a mound of curls piled on her head, and the smart silk dress flared wide at the hips in the way of the latest style. Before she sat, she leaned down and kissed Jean on both cheeks.

For a moment, Jean felt a bit like an imposter in his borrowed clothes. He hadn't changed since Eugene gave him a set of clothes. Though this was not unusual in a world where people usually had only one set of clothes, he could see that people of a higher class often had many sets of clothes. After having seen Michelle only in her nurse's gown for eight months, in the past week he had seen her wearing *four* different dresses.

"Mmmm! That looks good." Michelle eyed the sandwich.

Jean pushed it toward her. "Take it. I'm not really hungry." It felt good to give her something. What he really wanted to do was kiss her, but not politely on the cheeks.

"Oh, no. I can't," she said pushing it back to him. "Why don't you order one for me?"

Jean waved over the waiter and placed the order.

They sat enjoying each other's company but not certain what they should say to each other.

Finally, Jean spoke. He couldn't help it. So much had happened that day that he was brimming over with news. "I drew Napoleon today."

"Really?"

"Yes, Jean-Auguste and I went to the Palace of Versailles and spent the day sketching the First Consul at work." Jean pulled out his sketch pad and opened to his drawings of Napoleon.

"I have never met him," said Michelle as she looked at the drawings, "except that day in the hospital."

A surge of pride flowed through Jean. He had not only spent the day with the great general but had been there when important policy was made.

"I watched him make the decision to negotiate the freedom of the French soldiers trapped in Alexandria," said Jean.

"They let you listen in?" Michelle's sandwich arrived, and she took a bite.

"Well, I think they forgot that Jean-Auguste and I were there. We were sitting at our easels drawing when a messenger arrived with news of the British fleet approaching North Africa." Jean bit into his sandwich.

Michelle examined his drawings. "These are wonderful." She laughed in delight. "How were you able to capture his expressions? All I remember about him was that his face never stopped twitching."

Jean was pleased she noticed. "I draw fast." He waved his hand in swift motions, mimicking quick movements of a brush or pencil.

Michelle giggled. "My word, you are fast."

Jean basked in Michelle's praise. At that moment, it seemed as if he would never tire of her encouragement.

"It was really Jean-Auguste who suggested I draw today. Jacques-

Louis had intended me to just assist, but Jean-Auguste brought an easel for me."

She turned the page. "This is just incredible." In this drawing, Napoleon's chin jutted forcefully. His brow was knitted in thought and the muscles along his jaw were taut. "It looks exactly like a man who would take any risk to achieve greatness."

"And it wouldn't have happened if you hadn't arranged the whole thing," Jean said.

Michelle flushed. "Well, you're good, and it seemed silly to me that you would just go back to the army and be killed. You have too much talent."

Jean's face clouded. "I really felt lucky today as I listened to Napoleon and his ministers debate whether to try to rescue the soldiers stranded in Alexandria."

"What do you mean?"

Jean took a sip of coffee and wiped his mouth. "Well, at first, Napoleon wanted to just leave them to be massacred by the British, but one of his ministers kept pushing for him to find another solution." Jean drummed his fingers on the table. "Finally, Napoleon agreed and ordered that they negotiate with the British for free passage in exchange for giving up any claims on Egypt."

"So the men will be saved!"

"If the British agree," replied Jean. "It's just that the whole time I kept thinking that I could have been one of those men left behind. I had been on that expedition. It was just sheer luck that I was assigned to the artists well behind the front lines."

"Not luck, fate," said Michelle firmly. "You were meant to discover your destiny as an artist. Whatever I did to help you along was meant to happen. I am no more responsible than anything else. You were meant to study with Jacques-Louis David."

"Perhaps, but I can't help but think it was all an accident and that I could just as easily be somewhere else."

"No! Without your talent, nothing would have happened," said Michelle fiercely. She grabbed his hand and squeezed.

Jean looked down at her grasp. He didn't know how to respond.

Just as quickly, Michelle let go and took a bite of her sandwich.

After a few minutes, Jean spoke, "I owe my life to Alain."

Michelle conceded that this was true. She had seen just how near death he was when Alain carried him off the battlefield despite suffering his own horrible wound.

"It is my duty then," Jean began hesitantly. He wasn't sure if he should speak to her about this or if he was confiding more than she wanted to know.

"What, Jean?"

Jean tore at the crust of his sandwich. "Well." He paused again. "I've been thinking."

"About what, Jean?" she asked.

"About earning some money," he said quickly.

"Why? You are fed and have a place to sleep in the studio."

"I just need to," replied Jean.

"But why?" pressed Michelle.

Jean wanted to tell her but he didn't think she would be interested in his problems, or perhaps his problems would scare her away. He picked up his coffee and drank. "I'll figure it out. I always do."

The subject had left them in an awkward silence. Finally, Jean said, "I better go." He stood.

"Wait," said Michelle. "I'd like to help."

"I'll take care of it." He shrugged. "I've got to go."

Michelle touched his arm. "Maybe you have more family than you think." She stood as well. "Tomorrow is Sunday. You won't have any duties at the studio. The square in front of Notre Dame will be packed. It has become a thriving market since they closed the cathedral and rededicated it to Reason and then the Supreme Being. Now, it's part of the church again and performing masses. I bet you could earn some money drawing portraits."

Impulsively, Jean took Michelle in his arms and kissed her. At first, he felt her tense and resist. Then she relaxed and before Jean fully comprehended what he had done, the kiss was over.

Michelle backed away. A wide smile spread across her face, and her hand went up to cover it. She almost tripped on her skirt as she turned. "Oh, Jean!" And she was gone.

CHAPTER 16

Drawing Conclusions

Ants pouring forth from the small mound surrounding the entrance to their underground colony. That's what the crowd looked like as it poured out of the giant doors of Notre Dame. As a boy, Jean had had always been fascinated by the intensity and sense of purpose in the way ants went about their business. These churchgoers moved with a similar quickness and fluidity. Dressed in their Sunday best, they flowed out the doors in a quickly shifting group that Jean thought surprisingly elegant.

Jean hurried to set up along the edge and tacked his portrait of Michelle to one side, then he tacked a blank sheet to a plank attached to the easel. He tried to capture the movement of the churchgoers before they dispersed. He was entranced by their movement and their shifting in space and wished he knew just how to represent that on the page. Before he could think more on this, he was approached by a family who had just left Notre Dame and were wandering through the marketplace. Jean could tell by their dress that the man was a merchant of some sort. He looked prosperous. His wife and daughter were dressed

fashionably in silk dresses with lots of bows. They examined the portrait of Michelle carefully.

"Oh, Father," said the girl. "This is wonderful!"

"Would you like one of yourself?" the father asked his daughter.

"Oh, please!"

The father turned to Jean. "Could we have a portrait of our
daughter?"

"Yes, it will be one franc," replied Jean. He picked up his pencil.

Without a word, the man dug into his pocket and handed over the
coin. Jean began to sketch out the shape of the girl's face. She was about
ten years old. Her curls cascaded around her face, and she had a long
nose and thin lips. Beneath her smile was a square jaw, and her eyes
were wide, with delicate eyebrows arching over them. As Jean drew, he
thought how pretty all girls this young are. They hadn't yet matured,
and so still held a genuine openness, which life beats out of some
people. "Now, hold still, Monique," the mother told her daughter.

"Oh, Mama." Monique stood straight and tall while her father
stepped behind Jean and watched.

As Jean drew with quick, sure strokes, he thought of Marie, Alain's
daughter, and the look in her eyes. It was tired and careworn, but it had
an awareness that came from hardship. He compared Marie to David's
twin daughters. Even though they were around the same age as Marie,
they still projected the innocence that comes from living a sheltered
life. Their faces seemed to embody an almost frivolous carelessness. He
knew that Émilie and Pauline meant well, but they had no understanding of the difficulties that most people suffered in the world. Their
only concerns were the next tea party and whatever gossip was circu-
lating among their circle.

Jean felt a pang of guilt for being so harsh in his judgment of them.
It wasn't their fault, but he knew he could never fall for someone like

them. Settling for someone like Marie was also not possible. He had left that world, even though he felt he still had ties and obligations there. He knew that was why he was attracted to Michelle. He so admired her sacrifices to work in the battlefield hospital. She did not have to do that. It was her decision. She worked hard to help others, not just him. He had seen her take care of dozens of wounded soldiers, with real sensitivity. He only hoped that her concern for him went beyond just charity, because at this moment he knew that he was in love.

"You're not done are you?" asked the father.

Jean realized he was so lost in his thoughts that he had stopped drawing. "Oh, no," he stammered. "I was just thinking." He worked the page with renewed focus and put aside his thoughts about Michelle.

Within a few minutes, Jean finally said, "There! I believe it's finished."

"Quite so," exclaimed the father.

Monique came around and looked at the portrait. "Oh, it's wonderful!"

"Very nice," said the mother.

Jean rolled the portrait into a tube and tied the paper with string.

Later in the day, as the long shadows of the Notre-Dame Cathedral darkened the square, Jean folded his easel. He had been much more successful than he imagined. He had drawn twelve portraits and made fourteen francs. Two people liked his work so much they gave him a franc tip.

Jean wanted to go directly to Alain's apartment, but he needed to bring his equipment back to the studio first. It was a long walk across town, and he didn't think he would be able to make it to the apartment until late. He thought it better that he go first thing in the morning.

Before anyone had arrived at the studio Monday morning, Jean was out the door. He went straight to Alain's apartment building and found the landlord, who was also the proprietor of the butcher shop next door.

The floor of the shop was covered in sawdust to soak up the blood from butchering animals.

"I would like to pay the Marquand family's rent."

The butcher buried his meat cleaver into the wood block and pushed the scraps of fat onto the floor for his dogs to eat. "They're already paid up for the month," he said as he wiped his bloody hands on his apron. He was a large man with thick shoulders and muscled arms from carrying large pieces of meat.

"What about next month?"

Grrrrrr! The two brown-and-white spotted dogs fought over the hunks of fat. Jean made sure he kept his distance from them.

"Next month?" The butcher kicked the dogs. "Shut up!" He came over to the counter and lifted a ham down from a hook and sliced off a piece. "There is no next month." He handed Jean the slice of ham.

"Thank you."

"We'll all be gone by then." He pointed to something posted on the door of his shop. It was an eviction notice. The entire neighborhood had been condemned.

"Where will you go?"

The man pursed his lips and blew air out. "I guess I'll move to Orleans. I have enough money saved to begin again."

"And everyone else."

"Who knows?"

Jean's spirits sagged. His efforts to help were for nothing. Earning money to pay their rent wasn't going to save them.

"Do you know where the Marquands are going to go?"

"The street, I suspect." He turned back to the chopping block and yanked the cleaver from it.

Jean dug into his pocket. He set four coins on the counter. "I'd like to purchase a ham."

The butcher lifted a ham from a hook at the back of store. "Three francs."

"Also, a franc's worth of sausages." Jean pushed the money forward. "If you could send them up to the Marquand's, I'd appreciate it."

The butcher wrapped the sausages in a newspaper. "They'll go right up."

CHAPTER 17

Strolling with the First Consul

Clap! Clap!

"Wake up!"

"Grrrrrmpph." Jean rolled from his pallet to his feet. His hair stuck up in all directions. Drool smeared across his cheek and sleep encrusted his eyes. "What?"

Outside, it was still dark.

"You're going for a walk with my father," said Jules. He was dressed and energetic, like he had been up for hours after a good night's sleep. "For the life of me, I can't figure out what he likes about you, but he'll soon figure out you're a waste of time."

Jean rubbed his face. He poured water into the washing bowl and splashed water on his face. "Brrrrrr!"

"Move it!" Jules was on his way out the door. "And look sharp!"

Pulling on his boots and buttoning his pants, Jean ran to follow. He stumbled down the empty hallway outside the studio. Normally packed with artists, patrons, and hangers-on, the hallway echoed his footsteps.

Jules went through the door and let it slam in Jean's face.

"What is your problem?" shouted Jean as he pulled the door open.

Jules was already a hundred feet ahead and walking fast. "You are!" He spun around and yelled. "You don't belong here. You should be back in the army where you can be the cannon fodder you're meant to be."

Jean balled his hand into a fist.

"Don't even think of hitting me," threatened Jules. "I'll make sure you regret it for the rest of your short life." He began walking fast under the gray sky. The stars had already disappeared, but the streaks of dawn had not quite begun.

"Where are we going?"

"I already told you," said Jules. "And remember, I'm just doing this because he asked me to."

They strode purposefully through the Tuileries, almost a mirror image of the Louvre but completely abandoned, toward the Place de la Concorde. They quickly passed the hollow building that had yet to be cleaned up. Jean tried to imagine what it was like when the Tuileries Palace was still grand and King Louis XIV lived there before abandoning it for the Palace of Versailles.

"Pretty soon my father will realize he can't allow you to ruin his portrait of Napoleon just as a favor to Michelle. You have no talent for sitting or drawing, and his indulging of Michelle will have to stop."

Jean hurried to keep up with Jules, who walked with a fury. He couldn't understand what Jules had against him since the first moment they met at the café with Michelle. Did Jules really hate soldiers to the extent that he wouldn't even bother to get to know Jean?

Up ahead stood David beside the empty wreck that was the Tuileries Palace. He waved to the two young men.

"Jules, you can return to the studio and prepare it for work," said David to his son.

Jules nodded and turned on his heel.

"Good morning!" said David heartily, but the tumor kept his face immobilized, so Jean wasn't sure if the greeting was sincere or not. "Did you sleep well?"

"Fine," said Jean. After the verbal assault by Jules, he was wary of what David had in mind.

David spun around and waved his arms toward the once-grand Tuileries. "Do you know the story of this place?" asked David.

"No," replied Jean.

David pointed to the hulk. "When Louis XVI was expelled by revolutionaries from Versailles, he and his family were taken here. By then, the building had been abandoned for decades and was already a wreck. I visited Marie Antoinette here two months after the storming of the Bastille. The palace was a cavernous graveyard. It smelled of mold. There was no furniture. The wallpaper was peeling off the walls. The royal family lived here like animals in a zoo. They slept in the corner of a room on straw pallets. Citizens could come and watch them any time they cared. Then, the king was executed in January of 'ninety-three. It was terrible, but necessary."

Jean had heard some of this before, but listening to David tell it, the story felt different. David had been there and seen it all, while Jean was still too young to understand these affairs at the time.

"Did you know that the royal family almost escaped?"

"No." Jean wondered why David was telling him all this, but he enjoyed being brought into the great artist's confidence.

"They disguised themselves as servants and made it all the way to the German border." David shook his head. "Sadly, a peasant recognized Louis from his resemblance to his coin! Isn't that amazing? A coin!"

Jean smiled at the irony of the story.

"They were returned to the Tuileries. The brutality of this era was a horror." David pointed to an area covered in weeds that once had been a garden. "There was some of the worst of it. On August tenth in 'ninety-two, bells in Paris began to ring everywhere. The people left their homes and made their way to the palace in anger. They stormed the palace. The royal family escaped to the General Assembly hall near the Place de la Concorde. But here, more than a thousand people lay dead by the end of the day. The guards were massacred, and the palace was looted. This was when it was clear that the monarchy would not survive the revolution. It was less than a year later when Louis was guillotined."

Jean heard sadness in David's voice, which surprised him. He had known that David had been involved in some of the worst of it. David had been one of the deputies of the National Convention that sentenced the king to death. He had been second in command under Robespierre during the worst of the terror and had almost been sentenced to death himself when the Convention was outlawed. What kind of man could participate in such atrocities and then wax nostalgic of bygone times? A shiver went down Jean's spine. He knew that he would always be scarred by the violence of war. It would shadow him like a dark cloak. He could only wonder if David's memories affected him similarly.

"It was a terrible time," Jean said innocuously. He didn't want to endorse nor condemn David for his actions. The David he knew was not the man he had heard about.

"I am ashamed of what I did," the great painter admitted. "I was part of a mob that was intent on vengeance no matter who suffered." He stopped and looked up at the palace. The windows had been smashed, and soot where fires had burned blackened the façade. "I think that is why we need Bonaparte more than ever. We need someone to lead us and to guide us. Otherwise, we might deteriorate again into our worst."

The two were almost at the Place de la Concorde, the Square of Peace. Built forty years earlier, it was the largest square in Paris. It was then renamed the Place de la Révolution, and a guillotine was set in its center. Here was where Louis XVI and Marie Antoinette were executed, and Danton and Robespierre were guillotined after the fall of the Convention. Between 1793 and 1795, twenty-eight hundred were killed there. It was said that the smell of blood was so strong that a herd of cattle refused to cross the place.

Now, as they approached the square, a group of soldiers sat quietly on their horses in the emptiness of the early morning. Suddenly, one of the soldiers dismounted. It was Napoleon. He handed off the reins to another and dug his hands in his pockets and waited.

"Bonaparte! It is so good to see you," David called with a false heartiness. Jean could tell that David was afraid of the general.

"My friend, it is good to see you, too," said Napoleon. His face twitched, and his left eye blinked.

Jean dropped back a few steps behind David and allowed the painter and the general privacy.

Napoleon gazed around the square. Eight statues circled the square. A moat, fed by the Seine River, passed along the square's edge. "This will be the center of Paris. Spurs will run from east to west and north to south. These great avenues will show the world the greatness of France and its center, Paris."

Jean followed where Napoleon was pointing. The new avenue would go straight through the wooden buildings where the Marquand's lived, just as he had been told. Though he had kept his tongue the other day at the Palace of Versailles, he could not hold it any longer. "What will happen to the people who live there now?"

Napoleon turned and stared at Jean as if he was noticing him for the first time. "They will move, of course."

"But where? Those are their homes," pressed Jean.

"The boy doesn't know what he's talking about," David interrupted.

"Why do you care?" asked Napoleon.

"The family of a lieutenant in the Fifty-seventh Ligne lives there." Jean took a step forward. "He saved my life," he added.

Napoleon stood silently for a moment. His face twitched as if he were irritated. Then he waved over the captain of the guard. The two men whispered for a minute. Finally, Napoleon smiled. "They will be moved to the barracks by the Assembly. They will have rooms of their own and will receive the lieutenant's stipend." He then dug into his pocket and pulled out a ten franc note. "Here."

Jean took the ten franc note. "Thank you, First Consul, but you've done enough."

Napoleon waved him off and climbed back onto his mount. "We will talk again next week, Jacques-Louis," he said. "And we'll have time for a long walk then." The First Consul started to ride away, but then stopped. "Jacques-Louis."

"Yes?"

Napoleon patted the flank of his horse. "I want you to include Charlotte, my favorite horse in your painting."

David nodded.

Napoleon turned his mount and rode off.

David spit in disgust. "He won't sit for the blasted painting, but his horse will."

Jean watched the First Consul ride away in the distance. He was grateful to the man for helping him with his burden. He could not wait to write Alain and tell Jacqueline. "I'll go to the stables and draw the horse for you."

"It's not just the horse," said David. "It's horses in general. I've never really painted one. And this one has to be rearing on its hind legs." He shook his head. "How do we capture that kind of movement and make it look real?"

"I don't know," said Jean.

"I don't either."

The two men returned to the studio.

"On second thought," David suddenly said. "I just might have a solution."

CHAPTER 18

The Picture Clears

"I think Bonaparte should be looking directly at the audience," said Jean. "If he's looking at us and we're slightly behind him, it's as if he's leading the way." Jean shifted his body so that he was looking back over his shoulder. He knit his eyebrows and clenched his jaw.

"Keep quiet!" shouted Jules as he pointed his brush at Jean. He, his father and several other students were painting Jean astride the stepladder. "And lift the sword up higher."

"His face should show his determination to lead his people to victory and glory. It's not about the sword," Jean ignored Jules who was getting on his nerves. Ever since he came to the studio, Jules had been harassing him. He thought that they had reached some sort of accommodation after the visit to the colorman, but Jules's behavior since proved Jean wrong. In fact, Jules seemed to be getting more and more agitated every day, and seemed to be taking it out more and more on Jean.

"Give it up, soldier boy," ridiculed Jules with a smirk.

And he seemed to be directing more and more of his nasty remarks to him being a soldier.

"You're just something for us to draw," added Jules. "You don't know what you're talking about."

David set down his brush and looked up at Jean. "But if he's pointing his sword, it'll look silly," he said ignoring his son's rude behavior and actually engaging Jean's suggestion.

Jules walked up beside his father. "He's the worst model I've ever had to paint." He threw a brush across the room. The brush smacked against the wall and slid down to the floor. Everyone in the studio stopped and looked up.

He's having a tantrum like a two-year-old child, thought Jean.

"No, he isn't very good as a model," admitted David.

Jean felt his heart sink. It looked like Jules had finally found a way to get rid of him. If he couldn't do the job he was supposed to do, then they'd send him away.

"Come down, Jean," said David. He waved Jean over as if to speak in confidence.

"And pack your things," added Jules. He smiled with satisfaction.

"No, Jules," said David. "That's not what I meant. Jean, I want you to take Gabriel's place at his easel. And Gabriel."

"Yes, sir," said Gabriel, a student who had not said a word since Jean had arrived, but worked diligently if not particularly with inspiration.

"I'd like you to take Jean's place." He ran his hand through his hair as if he were trying to think of something.

"Yes, sir." Gabriel took off his paint smock and mounted the ladder. Jean handed him the bicorn, cloak, and sword.

"But, Father," said Jules. "He hasn't earned a place in your studio."

"Did you see his drawings of Bonaparte?" He gave Jean an encouraging smile.

Jean realized that Jules was not going to get rid of him, no matter how much Jules wanted him to go.

"Why, no," he stuttered. "But what does that have to do with it?"

"Jean, get your sketchbook."

Jean opened his sketchbook to the pages from the day he went with Ingres to Versailles. The drawings were strong. Each line held a sense of life and tension that suggested energy.

Jules grabbed the sketchbook out of Jean's hands. "He wasn't sent to draw. He was to be Jean-Auguste's lackey," protested Jules. He turned several pages back and saw a portrait Jean had done of Michelle. He stared at the portrait without saying a word. Then he slammed the book shut.

"He's much better than that," said Ingres from across the room.

"Was I talking to you?" spat Jules angrily at Ingres.

"Look!" his father ordered, taking the sketchbook from his son and flipping to the sketches of Napoleon.

Jules ignored the pages and walked out of the studio. The door slammed behind him.

"He'll be fine," said David, trying to explain his son's actions. "Eugene!"

"Yes, Father."

"Go after your brother. He will need you."

Eugene hurried after his brother.

The painters resumed their work. Jean was elated that he was on this side of the easel. He was no longer just a sitter. Though officially he had not been accepted as a student in David's studio, he certainly was allowed some of its privileges.

It felt like hours that Jean was allowed to share in this marvelous endeavor: doing painting studies. As he made his strokes on the page, trying to move beyond merely drawing with a paintbrush, he would surreptitiously glance around the room at David and the others. Though Jean couldn't see his work, he could tell that Ingres was working intensely. The young painter's hand moved with a sureness and confidence that Jean clearly lacked. Jean made a mental note that he could learn a lot from Ingres. Already, the young painter had encouraged and offered advice to Jean when the two visited Versailles. Jean was glad to have an ally, especially since he knew now that he had a real enemy in Jules.

After a while, David stopped working. He stood and strolled around the room looking at everyone's progress, picking and choosing among the ideas he was seeing. When he got to Jean, he noticed that Jean had not drawn the sword in Gabriel's hand. Instead, Jean had Gabriel pointing.

"That's it," said David. "Bonaparte would be pointing toward the St. Bernard Pass and toward the future." But he added, always the teacher, "Look at the muscle in that arm—your arm looks like a stick." He turned to the room. "I think we're nearly ready to begin the painting. I still have to work out the horse, but we can lay out the background. Everyone put away your materials. We'll start on the big canvas tomorrow morning."

At that moment, Eugene returned. "Jean," he called and handed Jean a note.

Jean opened it and read:

> My dear Jean,
> Please meet me at the café as soon as possible.
> Yours,
> Michelle

Jean cleaned up as quickly as possible and ran out of the studio.

"Jean, over here!"

Jean snaked through the tables and sat across from Michelle. "What's wrong?"

Michelle looked like she was crying. "It's Jules. He came to see me this afternoon."

"What about him? He stormed out of the studio earlier. David had allowed me to trade places with Gabriel. I worked behind his easel and he was the model. This seemed to anger Jules beyond reason, but I didn't think much of it since he hates me so."

"It isn't that he hates you so much as he hates that I like you," she said.

Jean didn't know what to say. He reached across and touched her hand. "Really?"

Michelle nodded.

"I...I like you, too."

Michelle smiled and wiped away a tear. "He has always thought that I would marry him ever since we were children, but I've always told him that I was not in love with him." She paused as if to gather strength. "And now that I've found someone I do like he has finally realized that what I've been saying all of these years might actually be true."

"Did you tell him this again today?"

She nodded.

"He'll get over it." Jean simply couldn't see Jules as being that vulnerable to anyone.

"I know, but I don't want to hurt him."

They sat in silence for a while, but it wasn't their usual awkward silence. It was like a kind of peace had settled between them. Occasionally, one would smile and the other would return the smile, but neither felt the need to break the power of the moment with words.

It was the waiter who broke the spell. "Would you care for anything?"

"Uh, no," replied Jean. In a flash he decided he wanted Michelle to meet Alain's family. "We're leaving."

"We are?" asked Michelle, surprised.

"I've got someone I want you to meet," said Jean as he took her hand and led her out of the café.

Soon they were at the Marquand's building, and as they climbed
the stairs to the second-floor apartment, he said, "I know you've met
Alain."

"Of course. He saved your life," she said remembering Alain's
devotion to Jean's recovery. "Is he all right?" Worry furrowed her
brow.

"Oh, yes!" Jean laughed. "I just want you to meet his wife and children. I have some really good news for them, and I thought you might
want you to share it with us."

"That is so wonderful of you, Jean." She squeezed his hand. "I
would love to meet Alain's family. I'm sure they're just as wonderful as
he is."

Jean and Michelle walked quickly.

When they reached the apartment, Jean knocked and Jacqueline
opened the door.

"Oh, Jean, please come in," she said. "Thank you so much for the
ham and sausages."

"Jean!" shouted one of the boys. Both little Alain and Girard
dashed across the room and hugged Jean around the waist.

"I loved the sausages!" shouted little Alain.

"I'm so glad," said Jean as he hugged the boys. "Now, let me introduce my friend." He turned to Jacqueline again. "This is Michelle
Durand. And Michelle, this is Jacqueline, Alain's wife. And these are
their sons, little Alain and Girard, and their daughter, Marie."

Marie was feeding coal into the stove's fire. "Hello!"

"Come," said Jacqueline. "We have plenty of ham. Please sit and eat."

Michelle looked at Jean who nodded that it was all right. They sat in
the apartment's two seats while the family looked on. A fresh baguette
lay in the center of the table.

Marie set a wooden board with a round of brie on the table. Jean picked up the knife and sliced through the white rind. The brie was ripe and spilled onto the board. Michelle tore the end off the baguette and dipped it into the gooey cheese.

"And we have plenty of ham left as well," added Jacqueline as she set slices of ham on the board.

"I didn't come to eat," protested Jean.

"I would be offended if you did not," replied Jacqueline.

"Thank you very much!" said Michelle. It was clear that she was hungry from the way she bit into a piece of ham.

"I came to tell you that I spoke with Napoleon." Jean swallowed a bite of cheese and bread. Once he tasted the good food, he realized that he, too, was hungrier than he had thought.

"You spoke to Napoleon!"

"Yes, and I have good news." Jean smiled widely. "You can all move into the officer's quarters next to the National Assembly. It has been arranged."

Jacqueline clapped her hands. "Jean, you have saved us!"

"Eat!" said Marie, wiping her eyes with her apron. "You are too skinny!"

"We'll see real soldiers every day?" asked Girard.

"Absolutely!" replied Jean. "Every day and every night, and even on Sundays!"

"I want to be a soldier!" shouted little Alain. "Just like Papa!"

Jean hugged little Alain. He knew that one day the boy would learn just how difficult a soldier's life really was. He thought of Alain with only half a hand and the possibility of not making it through the next battle. A shiver of relief moved through him. He was glad that his life had taken this turn. Until now, he had not had the perspective to understand just how terrible and arbitrary life in war really was.

CHAPTER 19

Rearing an Artist

Jean was stunned by how much the dazzling sunlight changed the colors on a canvas. At one moment, the painting might look dark and foreboding, but when the afternoon sunlight crawled across the canvas, the paint actually looked luminescent. It was as if light made color come alive. He had never thought about the effects of sunlight on the world before. In the past, when the sun shown, it was light outside; and when it didn't, it was dark. By looking closely at the paintings hung on the studio wall, Jean began to discover that there were all kinds of shades and intensities that the light in different times of day made possible. And as Jean watched David and the assistants build up layers of paint, he understood that color was created as much on the canvas as in the mixing on the palette.

It was an epiphany. He had been so obsessed with capturing the shading and line of something that he had completely overlooked how light actually made color.

Things were happening not only in the way he perceived, but also in the studio. One of the large blank canvases that Jean had sealed with rabbit-skin glue had been hung on the wall. The easels had been put away in a corner, and the drawings and studies that they had been doing for the past weeks were laid on a long table. Eugene, Ingres, and Gabriel worked on laying down the rudiments of the mountains as worked out in David's final paint studies.

Jean marveled at the complex step-by-step construction of this large painting. After weeks of discussion and sketching, always refined by David's hand, the assistants were beginning to paint in the base of the painting.

As David inspected what the three were doing, he suddenly barked, "Stop!" His face was crimson in anger.

Jean looked up from the table where he was uncorking a bottle of turpentine. He quickly tried to figure out what he might be doing wrong, but it wasn't him being yelled at.

"I can't believe we did this." David examined the canvas closely. He then picked up a pallet knife and stuck it in the canvas tearing the fabric. "How many times must I repeat 'fat over lean'?" He ripped the canvas further. "Fat over lean!"

"I…ah…" Ingres tried to explain himself.

"No! There's nothing you can say." He looked at all of them. "Any of you! If we hadn't caught this now, the painting would have become an embarrassment."

"Fat over lean?" repeated Jean. He didn't have a clue what David was talking about, but it was clear by the expressions on the faces of Eugene, Ingres, and Gabriel that they did.

David pointed at the canvas where the paint was drying incorrectly. He paced over to the table where the paints were. He picked up another palette knife and spread the azure on the table. "See the way this pools? See the rippling effect along the edges? What kind of oil was used with the pigment?" If the left side of David's face wasn't frozen by the tumor, he would be grimacing.

Everyone turned to Jean who had gone with Jules to the colorman.
"I'm not sure," said Jean. "I think linseed."

"What kind of linseed?" asked David. "Azure normally has low oil
content, but this looks like the pigment is suspended in a lot. Where's
Jules?"

"You know he hasn't been around since he ran out last week,
Father," replied Eugene. "He's disappeared." Jules had not returned to
the studio since his outburst. Jean was surprised, but relieved that he
hadn't seen him. He was not looking for another confrontation, especially after learning about his feelings for Michelle.

"He ordered the paints," added Ingres. "He's usually the one who
makes sure the paints with heavy oils go underneath." Ingres was
describing the "fat over lean" concept, which meant that paints that
had a lot of oil and little thinner like turpentine dried slower than
paints with less oil or paint mixed with thinner. If a slow-drying paint
was laid underneath a fast-drying paint, the paint would crack and
sometimes would even flake off. "If Jules had been around, this
wouldn't have happened."

"I should know," said Jean. "I was there."

David pointed at Eugene. "Now this is your responsibility. Find
out from Viggo what kind of linseed oil was used. The consistency
looks sun-thickened." David started out the studio and then turned.
"Prepare a new canvas. And Jean?"

"Yes," he said nervously. He wished he had understood, or even
just listened to, what Jules had been ordering. Then maybe he would
not be yelled at now.

"Come with me." Jean followed David out. He was expecting to be
reprimanded, but instead David's tone was gentle and friendly. "Go
back and get a lantern. I want to show you something."

Jean returned with a lantern. He had stopped by the stove and lit the wick. "Where are we going?" He held the lantern away from his side so that he wouldn't burn himself.

"The basement," said David.

"There's a basement?" asked Jean.

"There's always a basement," laughed David. "That and in attics is where treasures are hidden." He opened a door at the end of the hall. It led down a flight of stone stairs. Jean was surprised to find the cellar was as large as a warehouse, with high ceilings. There were rows of shelves and lamps hanging from the rafters.

"Light the lamps on this end," said David as he looked from shelf to shelf for something. "Have you heard of Étienne Maurice Falconet?"

"No," said Jean as he wiped a cobweb from his face and lit the last lamp. The room had an eerie glow to it.

"Étienne died back in 'ninety-one. He was a great sculptor. The Louvre had five of his sculptures, half the work of his lifetime. But the one we're looking for today is only a wax model. The original is in Russia...in St. Petersburg."

David rummaged around for a little bit until he looked under a piece of canvas draped over a large object about four feet high. "Ah! Here we are!" He pulled the canvas off the object, and a dark wax sculpture of a man on a rearing horse appeared. "This is Falconet's famous *Peter the Great*."

Jean moved closer to inspect it.

"Keep the lantern away. We don't want to melt it," said David. "This is the model for the finest equestrian statue ever made."

Jean examined the four-foot-high wax sculpture of Peter astride a rearing horse on the edge of a cliff. "It is beautiful," Jean said reflexively, then regretted his words because to him they sounded so predictable.

"Yes, it's quite magnificent!" David ran his hand along the horse's flank. "The equestrian monument has presented the sculptor with a formidable problem. It involves the balance of a vertical element on a large horizontal mass, which in turn rests on very slender supports; and this problem leads to another, that of combining the two forms into a structural unity. Nearly all equestrian statues are portraits—portraits of a special kind, because the character of the rider may be suggested by that of his mount. The horse at rest evokes a sense of authority, the rearing horse implies the man of action."

"And you want Bonaparte to be a man of action?"

"Exactly! Etienne studied the best horses in the royal stables. Day after day, he had riding masters gallop at great speed onto a specially constructed model of the pedestal. He then copied the movements and poses as quickly as he could with his pencil. After hundreds of attempts, he finally found a way of depicting the horse."

Jean ran his hand along the horse. "It's like I can feel the muscles straining under the skin."

"That's the key to doing it right. You have to make it feel like the flesh is alive, and in order to do that you have to understand—actually see—what is underneath before you can paint what is on top." David re-covered the model with the fabric.

"Should we be studying horses at the stables?"

" First, I want you to bring this upstairs to the studio," he explained. "Get Eugene to help you."

Later, outside Boisvert Military Hospital, Jean paced. He knew that Michelle worked that day, and he just had to see her. He had to speak with her. No, he had to kiss her. He did not think he could survive the day without feeling her lips pressed to his. Ever since the other night when she accompanied him to the Marquand's to deliver the good news, he finally trusted that she could be his. What that meant, he wasn't certain. He wasn't even officially an artist's apprentice. He had not made a name for himself and had no means to make a living. But he did belong in David's studio and was now a step beyond simply being the sitter for Napoleon's portrait, even if he wasn't officially an apprentice. As well, he wasn't studying with just any painter, but Jacques-Louis David, the anointed artist of the revolution. This had to weigh in his favor, especially since it was Michelle's support that got him to this place.

As Jean ran all these possibilities through his mind, wondering if Michelle really was as attracted to him as was he to her, he nervously walked up and down the block. He couldn't stand still.

As the evening's darkness descended, men started lighting the street lamps. As time passed, Jean worried that he had somehow missed her. He watched each time the door to the hospital opened, hoping that it would be her, only to be continually disappointed. The longer he waited, the more anxious he became. In the back of his mind he questioned whether she had changed her mind or not meant what she said. A sudden rush of doubt washed through him. Maybe she no longer worked at the hospital. Maybe she never told him she quit because she didn't think it was important to share that with him. The longer he stood there waiting for her, the more foolish he began to feel. As the minutes ticked away, he became certain that she had moved on and hadn't told him. He knew for a fact that he would never see her again.

The hospital door swung open, and finally there was Michelle.

Jean's heart seemed to skip a beat. "Michelle!"

She looked up at the sound and saw Jean standing at the bottom of the stairs.

As all his anxieties burst forth, Jean immediately launched into all he wanted to tell her.

"You won't believe what happened today," continued Jean. "I saw Falconet's wax model of *Peter the Great*. It's going to be perfect in helping us with Napoleon's portrait. Did you know that his sculpture is the only sculpture that really captures the muscles and movement of a horse rearing?"

Michelle descended wordlessly.

"It was just amazing," Jean continued breathlessly. "And tomorrow I'm going to the stables to see Napoleon's horse." Jean couldn't stop talking, he was so excited. "We had a problem with the paints though." He held out his arms to embrace her.

Michelle stared at him coldly. "I don't have time to talk."

"But...but..." stammered Jean. "The paints..." He arms fell to his side.

Michelle pushed past him. Then she abruptly turned. "Listen, Jean." She paused and waved her hand. "Never mind." She ran down the street, crying.

Stunned, Jean slowly sat on the hospital steps. "It was a mistake," he muttered. "I shouldn't have brought her to meet Alain's family. They scared her away. It reminded her where I come from, and that I could never really enter her world. Her father is a doctor. Mine is a dead soldier. Her mother probably spends her days having tea. My mother was a laundress who died when I was still a boy." He rubbed his hand over his face to wipe away the tears. "I was fooling myself." He stood and headed down the street in the opposite direction from the way Michelle went.

CHAPTER 20

A Stable Friendship

Holding a riding crop in his hand, the cavalry horse trainer stood next to Jean by the fence of the riding ring. He raised the crop and snapped it. "Piaffe!" he shouted to the cavalry officer riding Napoleon's white stallion.

The horse sprung forward as if in sudden advance. The stallion's mane flew out as its hooves momentarily curled underneath its broad chest. The bay landed with a snort and raised its head proudly.

"This move is important during battle. The quick movement surprises the enemy," explained the trainer. The stallion circled the ring in a clipped trot. Its muscles seemed as fluid as a brook running over smooth stones.

"Levade!"

The horse made a highly collected half-halt and dipped slightly as the rider slashed his hand downward as if he held a sword. The rider and horse seemed to move as a single being with strength and speed.

"This is the ideal move when you want to slash an enemy on foot," said the trainer. He pointed at the rider and horse. "See how the rider is in position to put his weight into the strike."

Jean nodded. He had heard of the extensive training that cavalry horses go through, but had seen little of it because he had been in the infantry.

"It was developed by one of the founders of the School of Versailles in 1729. Perhaps the greatest master of cavalry training, Robichon de la Gueriniere wrote the book that everyone uses, *Ecole de Cavalerie*. He initially designed the move for use with small arms that had just become common in battle. Then he discovered that it also was an ideal defensive tactic and made many an enemy miss."

As Jean watched, he tried to decide how he could possibly draw a horse frozen on the page when it was in constant movement. Unlike drawing a person, a horse could not be stilled or posed. This required a quick hand and an ability to visualize what was no longer in sight. He remembered what David had said when he described Falconet having someone ride the horse repeatedly up a ramp and have him rear. Jean thought that might be the only solution.

"Pirouette!" shouted the trainer. The crop snapped again.

The rider wheeled around to the right and to the left. Jean could see the sweat forming on the stallion's shoulders as it worked.

"This action is perfect when one needs to move away from or toward the enemy from a surprising angle." The trainer smiled. "He is such a lovely horse. Such beautiful lines and grace. Courbette!"

The stallion rose on its hind legs rearing high into the air. The horse's hind hooves stutter-stepped forward as the rider kept his balance on horse's back.

"Here, the rider can disperse foot soldiers easily. Capriole!"

The stallion made a giant leap into the air. Jean could imagine the horse leaping over a stone wall that marksmen might be hiding behind.

"A horse and rider can escape over the heads of the infantry with a leap this high."

"That is amazing!" exclaimed Jean. He dug out his sketchbook and propped it on the top of the fence surrounding the riding ring. "But what I need is more of the courbette. That's what David wants in his painting."

The rider circled the ring again and performed a series of repeated courbettes. It was dizzying to watch the horse extend so high into the air on its thin ankles and legs. In some ways it seemed against the law of gravity for such a heavy beast to be balanced on two small hooves.

Instinctively, Jean's hand started to move across the paper. Seeming more like mere scribble, he was actually recording masses of muscles, direction of thrust, tension of line, a record of the horse in movement.

"Jacques-Louis will be here later to draw. If you could arrange to have several horses and riders available so that he and his students could draw, that would be wonderful."

"We will be ready," replied the trainer. He brought the crop down and swatted his thigh. The rider settled the horse and rode out of ring.

Jean and the chief trainer shook hands.

"Damn!" The invective came from behind Jean and was blurted in such an emphatic burst that Jean automatically spun around.

The person who had sworn had slipped into a stall in the stable. Still, Jean recognized the voice. The tone of anger was something he had become familiar with over the past few months at David's studio. He was surprised to hear it in the military compound.

"Jules!" Jean trotted after the shadow.

Behind stacked bales in the stall, Jules crouched like a frightened child.

"Uh, Jean, what a surprise," said Jules as he stood.

Jean was at a loss for words. Seeing Jules kneeling there, so unsure of himself, stunned Jean. He simply stared at David's eldest son wearing the uniform of a lieutenant in the cavalry. "Where did—?"

"I was called up," muttered Jules as he looked down at his shoes.

"Called up?" repeated Jean, wanting more of an explanation. Jean's mind was spinning. Immediately, anger rushed to the forefront. How could a worm like Jules become a lieutenant without any experience, when it had taken Alain years to reach that rank? And Alain had earned it in battle, while Jules had been given the rank solely because of his social position. Jean wanted to rip the epaulets off of Jules's shoulders.

"Well." Jules took a deep breath. It seemed like it was taking all of his strength to speak, which struck Jean as strange since Jules had always seemed to exude power. "I was going to be conscripted, so I joined the cavalry. I've always been good with horses. In fact, I was able to bring my own horse, Lightning." He patted the flank of the horse in the stall.

"Does your father know?" asked Jean, trying to control his anger until he figured out what was going on. He couldn't believe that no one had spoken about it in the studio. The nature of working such long hours together in the studio had made it nearly impossible for anyone to keep a secret from the others.

"No," said Jules. "I was going to write him once I arrived at the Rhine." He grabbed a brush and started to groom his horse. "The Second Coalition looks like it's collapsing, so we're being sent to guard against an Austrian incursion." He nervously bit his lip.

"You can't do this!" Jean entered the stall. "You don't deserve to be a lieutenant when you haven't even earned it." The horse snorted and kicked the stall.

The two young men stood and stared at each other. Neither said a word nor moved.

Finally, Jean tried to take another approach. "Your father can get you out of this. He needs you." He crossed his arms.

Jules glared angrily. "No! I must do this."

Jean grabbed Jules by the sleeve and tried to pull him from the stall.

"You can't fight. You don't know the first thing about fighting."

"Let go! I have to do this," spat Jules as he pulled himself from Jean's grip. "Besides, I can learn. You did." He stood his ground stubbornly.

"No, you can't," yelled Jean angrily. "You don't know what you're getting yourself into."

"Oh, because I didn't grow up in the camps like you?" snapped Jules.

"You idiot! Most recruits don't last the first five minutes of battle. Do you remember that night at the café when I first met you?"

"Yes."

"Well, you were right when you said we were cannon fodder." Jean couldn't believe that he was actually admitting that what Jules had said was true. So much had changed over the last few weeks. He had learned just how little Napoleon really cared for his soldiers and how expendable they were to him. With what Jean now knew, he wouldn't let his worst enemy go to the front.

"People of officer class have superior blood," Jules said haughtily. "We survive because we are better than everyone else."

Jean stared at Jules. "Are you really that stupid?"

Jules paused for a moment and caught his breath. "Just promise me one thing."

"Promise what?"

"That you'll take care of Michelle." A tear rolled down Jules's cheek.

Jean was stunned by Jules's sudden display of emotion. A moment before, he had been an arrogant fool. And in the past, he had acted like a bully. Now, he seemed not just uncertain, but heartbroken. This was the Jules he had witnessed attending to his father, not the Jules he knew as an adversary. Jean was aware that Michelle was close to Jules, but he had always thought her feelings were platonic with respect to Jules.

"Like she'd listen to an uneducated sewer rat like me," said Jean bitterly. He couldn't help himself. The mention of Michelle left Jean feeling hurt and confused.

Jules stomped his foot, and the horse skittered to the left. Jean stepped back out of the stall. He was afraid of being trampled.

"She won't even speak to me," Jean whispered.

"You've got to make sure she's all right, no matter what!"

"I will," said Jean, not wanting to explain how much things had changed between Michelle and him, but very much wanting to end this as quickly as possible.

"Or I'll come back and kill you," added Jules.

The two young men stared at each other again until Jules finally looked away.

"I've got to go," said Jules as he pushed past Jean.

"No! The studio can't function without you!" Jean then remembered what happened with the paints. "What kind of oil was used in the medium?" he shouted to the empty stable.

CHAPTER 21

Relapse at the Hospital

Jean returned to a studio busy with the work of preparing to paint a grand work of art.

Around the studio, smaller paintings were nearing completion. Each of these painting studies explored an aspect of the larger painting—clumps of soldiers, artillery pieces, studies of Napoleon's face, with some looking like the First Consul and others stripped of his distinctive features.

Jean immediately approached David, who was looking over Ingres's shoulder. "I've arranged for you to draw the horses tomorrow."

"Good," muttered David, not looking up.

Jean hesitated. He struggled to decide whether to tell the master painter about his son Jules. He really didn't want to be the bearer of such news.

David felt his presence. "What is it?"

"Er...." Jean tried to think of something to say. "I made some drawings."

David held out his hand. "Let's see."

Jean handed him the sketchbook, and David took over to the long worktable.

After studying the pages, David said, "I can feel the physical weight of the horse."

"This is exactly how we can capture the horse's vitality," continued David. "Simply studying the Falconet model will not get us all the way there. We must understand the energy and strength of the animal in order to demonstrate the power of the man astride the horse."

Jean basked in David's praise, putting all of his misgivings about not speaking of Jules aside. He did not want to risk losing his newly earned respect by bringing bad news to David.

"This kind of drawing brings us closer," added David, "much closer."

Like swallowing a mug of some particularly foul medicine, Jean reluctantly went to Boisvert Military Hospital. He had nowhere else to turn. He just couldn't let David find out in a letter from Jules. By then it would be too late. At the same time, Jean was afraid that if the news came from him, he might be thrown out. He didn't want that, but he also knew that David needed his son to run the studio. Without Jules, things seemed to fall apart. The incident with the paint was only one of several problems that arose since Jules had disappeared. Worst of all, the discipline of the David's students was becoming a problem, and David was not good at giving them direction. The master artist had come to depend on his son to ensure that everything ran smoothly. Though Eugene was trying to pick up the slack, he shared of his father's knack for disorganization.

The only person he could go to was Michelle. No matter how angry she might be at him, he had to convince her to help. She could speak to Jules and convince him that the cavalry was not where he was needed. She could tell David without there being any repercussions for Jean.

She was the only person he could turn to. As he walked across town, he became more and more desperate to find her. His pace quickened until he was almost at a dead run.

He weaved his way through the busy city, dodging carts and carriages and scooting around slower pedestrians. In the middle of the next block were the steps to the hospital. He hurried along the uneven cobblestones, intent on getting there before Michelle left for home. Taking two at a time, he climbed the stairs and entered the hospital foyer. The familiar face of the guard at the admitting desk broke into a smile when he looked up and saw Jean coming in.

"Long time."

"I've been kind of busy," replied Jean.

"No reason to apologize," replied Claude as he shuffled some papers on the desk. "If you leave here alive, it's better not to return."

"Has Michelle Durand left?"

Claude glanced up the stairs. "I don't understand why she keeps returning. She has so much to live for. She could be going to parties and entertaining handsome men, but she comes here and tends to those who won't live out the month."

Jean scuffed his boot on the marble floor. "I'm not sure either, but she helped me get out of here, so I can only be grateful to her."

"Get out of here." Claude waved Jean away.

Jean started to climb the stairs, stunned by his words to Claude. Michelle had hurt him, but the first words to spill from his mouth were his gratitude. *Where did that come from?* he wondered.

"So, tell her that you love her already!" shouted Claude after him.

The clink of metal on metal, the moan and cries of men suffering, the whispers of doctors and nurses, the footsteps of orderlies—all echoed down the hallways and spilled into the stairwell. Jean didn't find that he missed these sounds. Instead, they felt like a long lost memory from the distant past. With each step, his heart leaped upward toward the floor and the ward where Michelle worked…where she tended to the sick…where she breathed the same air as he and a hundred others, but most important, her breath and his were linked by air…air that circulated between them, uniting them, joining them, even making their separation.…

Jean laughed at his silliness. "Come to your senses," he scolded himself. "She can't be really interested in you. You're not here to win her over. You're here to help Jules. You need Jules to help his father. Michelle is the only person who can convince Jules to return to the studio. You need her help one more time. Be grateful she got you the job in David's studio and don't expect anything else."

On the fourth-floor landing, Jean felt a lump in his throat. He wanted to cough and dislodge it, but the feeling wouldn't go away. To muster courage, he reminded himself that he had faced worse when he faced an enemy that fired real bullets and cannonballs. How could Michelle's disinterest compare to that? He had to admit it couldn't, but somewhere deep down he would rather face a thousand charges against an enemy army encampment than admit that his chances with Michelle were nonexistent. No matter how many times she might tell him she liked him, Jean knew that they could never truly be together. She was an educated Parisian, while he was simply an orphan of the army.

As he hesitated on the fourth-floor landing, trying to find that courage somewhere inside him, the door to the amputee ward swung open.

"Oh!" Michelle walked directly into Jean.

"Oh!" repeated Jean. "It's you." He forced a smile, ready to kick himself for such lack of imagination.

They stood before each other warily.

After a moment, Michelle turned away. "I have to go."

"Wait!" blurted Jean awkwardly. "We need to speak."

"I don't have anything to say to you." She backed into the ward.

Jean followed. "Yes, we do. I just left Jules. Did you know he joined the cavalry?"

"And you didn't have something to do with that?" Michelle began tucking in a sleeping patient's sheets.

"I didn't."

"Of course." Her reply dripped with disbelief. "Do you think Jules would do this on his own? He hated the army." She slammed her hands down on the bed.

"Uggggghhh!" moaned the patient.

"Oh, I'm sorry." She adjusted the patient's pillow and then turned on Jean. "If you hadn't made him feel an inch tall, he wouldn't have felt the need to prove himself by joining the cavalry."

"Me?" Jean stepped back as if he had just received a blow. "I didn't do anything."

"And you took advantage of my confidences!" A strand of hair fell over her face. Jean couldn't help but be distracted by it.

"What?"

"I told you that I liked you and not Jules," ranted Michelle. "You used that knowledge to make Jules feel even smaller. Without me and no other place to go, he joined the cavalry." She marched across the aisle to another bed and started to tuck more sheets.

"Uh, I'm fine," said the patient. "I don't need your help—ouch!"

"Oh." Michelle put her hand to her mouth when she realized she was practically tying the patient to the bed.

"I swear. Jules and I never talked until today. I didn't know he had joined up," Jean blurted, desperate to make things right.

Michelle stopped. "You didn't know?"

"No!"

"But he wouldn't have done this if he wasn't somehow competing with you. When I heard he had joined, I just assumed you were behind it somehow." Tears brimmed in her eyes, but she held them back. "Oh, what a fool I've been."

"No, you haven't." Jean came to her side and held her. He wanted to brush the tears away. He wanted to kiss her eyes. He took out his handkerchief and dabbed her cheeks. "I swear I didn't do anything. I wouldn't send my worst enemy into the army, especially after listening to how willing Napoleon is to sacrifice soldiers. When Dominique and I were sketching him at Versailles, he seemed just as capable of leaving a division stranded in Alexandria at the mercy of the British, as not." Just remembering the experience of powerlessness in that circumstance made his heart race.

Michelle stared at him a long minute. A short nod followed, as if she had suddenly made up her mind. "Okay, but what can we do?"

"We have to go to his father," explained Jean. "Napoleon will listen to him. All he has to say is the studio can't be run without Jules."

"It has to work," she insisted as she pounded her fist into the palm of her other hand.

CHAPTER 22

Owning Your Actions

The wind picked up off the Seine in the early morning air and sent a chill through the parties who stood among the ruins of the Tuileries Palace. Leaves rustled like nervous children before the start of school.

Jean dug his hands deep in his pockets as he listened to Michelle explain to David what his son Jules had done. Jean played with a coin buried in the pocket. The cool metal was calming to his mixed emotions.

"It was impulsive," said Michelle, "and it was my fault." Her brown curls lifted in the wind, forming a halo around her bonnet.

"Don't be silly," replied David with a dismissive wave of his hand. He turned his collar up and buttoned his coat. His tumor had flushed a bright red.

"You know how Jules feels about me," said Michelle, "and you know that I don't feel the same about him." Her face had a pained look.

David smiled. "All young men experience unrequited love. Why I remember...."

"That's not the point," insisted Michelle. "I've hurt him, and now he's put himself in danger."

"But why do this?" said David with bewilderment. "He hates war."

"He hates soldiers, too," added Jean. "He told me as much when we first met."

"No," admitted David. "What he hated was *you*."

"You must stop him," pleaded Michelle. "You could get him released for his commitment to run the studio."

David thought as he walked toward the Place de la Concorde. "Perhaps."

"You said it yourself," said Jean. "You need Jules. The studio is a mess without him."

"Well, I'll see what I can do," said David. "Follow me." The three crossed the palace grounds and entered the square. "Bonaparte and I are to go walking this morning."

At the edge of the square, Napoleon stood beside his horse, talking to one of the captains of his escort.

"Ah, Jacques-Louis!" He waved to the painter. "There you are. I thought you might have forgotten."

"No, my friend. I was trying to decide what to do about my son."

"Your son? What has happened?" Napoleon took off his bicorn hat and held it over his heart.

"Jules has joined the cavalry." The men kissed each cheek in greeting.

"The cavalry is a fine place for a young man," replied Napoleon. He handed the reins of his horse to the captain.

David and Napoleon made their way across the square, with Jean and Michelle following behind.

"Yes, most certainly, but I need Jules to manage my studio," explained David. "I don't think I can finish your portrait without him."

"I see," said Napoleon as he rubbed his chin. Even in moments of contemplation, the First Consul's face could not rest. The right eye twitched, and the corners of his mouth grimaced and relaxed almost to the rhythm of a ticking clock.

The two men walked in silence down a street that would become one of Napoleon's grand thoroughfares crossing north to south. Jean looked at Michelle questioningly. She shrugged. Neither would speak for fear of disrupting the moment. Everything depended on how Napoleon responded. He could ignore David's plea or he could help him. It was all within the power of the First Consul.

Jean knew that David could not explicitly asked for Jules to be released from his military obligation. That would put Napoleon in an awkward position, which might jeopardize not just Jules, but David as well. They could not risk embarrassing the First Consul. The decision had to come from Napoleon so that he could appear both generous and fair.

As time clicked away, Jean became more and more alarmed. He thought about how indifferent Napoleon seemed to saving his own soldiers and wondered if the life of a single young man would be of any interest to him.

Finally, a smile spread across Napoleon's face. "There's something I've been thinking about lately."

"And what is that?" asked David.

"I've been thinking that I would like more copies of my portrait painted. Charles IV of Spain is getting the first one, but I will need the painting as well, several in fact. The people will want to see it, and we'll need to get it around the country." He stopped and turned to David.

Jean could tell that Napoleon had something more in mind than just making copies, but what he didn't know.

"I think the painting will help my cause."

"And what cause might that be?" asked David.

"Why, the French empire, of course."

"Of course," repeated David. "And more versions of *Bonaparte Crossing the Alps at St. Bernard* would help that cause?"

"Quite precisely."

"And if I agree to these additional canvases?"

"I might be able to find a way to release your son from the service," said Napoleon.

Jean caught his breath. Napoleon was finding a way to give David what he wanted without losing face. At this moment, Jean realized just how good a general Napoleon actually was. The First Consul could negotiate something even as trivial as Jules's freedom in a way that benefited him. Jean knew that David would agree to this. The great painter had no choice. Napoleon had cornered the man.

"And my payment for these paintings would be?" asked David.

"Well, Charles IV is paying you twenty-four thousand francs for the first one. The other three won't be nearly as difficult to duplicate." He walked onward. David followed a step behind and then caught up. "I would say that seven thousand francs for each additional painting would be sufficient recompense."

"Ten thousand francs," said David.

Napoleon eyed the painter and nodded his ascent.

Michelle reached out and squeezed Jean's hand. "He did it," whispered Michelle.

As Jean looked into her face, he could tell that whatever tension had been between them was long forgotten. "Of course, he did. He is Jacques-Louis David."

CHAPTER 23

The Last Stroke

"There!" said David as he set down his brush and gazed at the final portrait. "Charles IV of Spain will certainly like this."

At the center of the wall hung *Bonaparte Crossing the Alps at St. Bernard*. The large painting dwarfed everything in the studio. It rose above the litter of drawings, painting studies, and Falconet model. The other paintings hanging on the walls seemed small and insignificant in comparison, though prominent amid the clutter were Jean's movement studies from the stables.

Jean and the others gathered around David as they gazed at the work.

"It's magnificent," offered Jean. "The horse seems about to leap off the canvas." Jean was amazed at how David had managed to bring Napoleon and the horse to the foreground while making everything else in the far distance.

"There's no middle distance in the painting," observed Ingres.

"Exactly," said David. "Napoleon must appear to be ahead of everyone. He is leading us to greatness, and nothing can compete with him." He crossed his arms in satisfaction.

"And that is the problem," added Jules.

Jean turned to him, waiting for an explanation. Since Jules had returned to the studio, he and Jean had come to a kind of truce. In fact, Jean imagined that perhaps sometime in the future they might even become friends, but he knew that that was well into the future. Jules still could not get over his resentment that Jean had won Michelle's heart over him.

"When Father painted heroes of antiquity, the message was that perhaps we could aspire to the greatness of the past. Before that, painters only celebrated the glory of God. Now, Father is suggesting that with Napoleon, we have this greatness before us in flesh and blood. It seems to me that exalting someone before history can determine his greatness is dangerous. What if he lets us down?"

The studio remained silent after Jules's words of caution.

Finally, Jean took a deep breath. "But the painting is wonderful." As he gazed at the balance of composition and the luminescence of painting technique in the portrait, he knew that this painting was something that would be remembered throughout history.

Jules went over and pulled an empty canvas of identical size out and set it beside the original. "We might as well begin the copy."

As David approached the blank space, he waved his hand and said, "This time I want the horse to be a bay, like my son's favorite horse." He smiled at Jules, and his son smiled back. Then he turned to Jean and said, "Now, Jean?"

"Yes, sir."

"Your job as a sitter is over." He paused.

Jean held his breath. He was afraid this meant that he would have to leave.

"Instead, you are officially an apprentice in the studio of Jacques-Louis David."

"Thank you!" Jean let out his breath, confident that for the first time he knew where he was meant to be.

As everyone congratulated Jean, the door at the back of the studio slammed open, interrupting the celebration. Michelle rushed through.

"Oh, Jean!" She looked as if she were about to cry. She held out a letter. "This came to the hospital by mistake."

Jean took the envelope and opened it. A worn scrap of paper with a barely legible scrawl was inside. Jean walked over to the window where he could see it better in the light. Before he even read the first word, he knew what it said. It seemed inevitable. Life was becoming just too good to be true.

> My Dearest Jean,
> I just received the news. Alain has died along the Rhine. A sniper's bullet took his life. I knew that you would want to know immediately.
> Yours,
> Jacqueline

Jean let the letter slip from his hand. David rushed over and picked it up. Michelle wrapped her arms around Jean and laid her head on his shoulder.

"Oh, Jean." David embraced his new pupil and Michelle, as Jean fought to hold back his tears.

Jacques-Louis David's Life and Art

At the end of the eighteenth century and the beginning of the nineteenth—an entire generation—no other artist ruled so supremely in Europe as Jacques-Louis David (pronounced zhåk-lw ee dåv ee d). He not only founded the neoclassical school of painting and became teacher to some of the greatest artists of the next generation, but his influence determined the course of fashion, furniture design, and interior decoration. His painting students included such masters as Jean-Auguste-Dominique Ingres, Francois Gérard, Antoine-Jean Gros, and Anne-Louis Girodet de Roussy-Trioson.

Born to a prosperous Parisian family on August 30, 1748, David's father Louis-Maurice was a merchant, who at nineteen married eighteen-year-old Marie-Genevieve Buron. When David was nine, his father was killed in a duel. His mother then sent him to live with his uncles, who were prosperous architects. An indifferent student, David loved to draw from an early age. He once said, "I was always hiding behind the instructor's chair, drawing for the duration of the class." As a boy, he developed a tumor on his face that made his speech slur for the rest of his life.

Despite his family's objections, he convinced them to allow him to study art. He initially went to work with François Boucher, a family friend and acclaimed rococo painter. Boucher sent David to study with his friend Joseph-Marie Vien, who embraced the classical reaction to the old-fashioned rococo style of the early seventeenth century. David attended the Royal Academy, which was located in what is now the Louvre. During his years of study he competed four times for the Prix de Rome, which was a scholarship to study at the French Academy in Rome. After losing three times, he finally won in 1774, at the age of twenty-six. He traveled to Rome with Vien, who was taking over as director of the academy.

While in Italy, David discovered a real love for Italian and Roman art and sculpture. He was particularly affected by classical sculpture and filled his sketchbooks with drawings of Pompeii and other Roman ruins, as well as the Renaissance masters.

After five years in Rome, David returned to Paris and became a member of the Royal Academy. In 1781, two of his paintings were included in the Salon of that year, which was one of the highest honors of the age. After the Salon, the king granted David lodging in the Louvre, one of the highest privileges an artist could earn. This honor, however, came with strings attached. In order to move into his new lodgings he had to agree to marry Marguerite-Charlotte, the daughter of the king's contractor of buildings. By this time, David had between forty and fifty students. He was commissioned by the government to paint *Horace Defended by His Father* and returned to Rome with his wife. While there, he painted *The Oath of Horatii*, which marked an important evolution in French painting. In *The Oath*, David sought to depict what he imagined were the "eternal" concepts of classicism. These included the portrayal of idealized virtue, perfection, and moral certitude. In his quest for perfection, David stripped away sentiment and emotion from his work. *The Oath* and the paintings to follow were a sudden and dramatic break from tradition, and many scholars mark this as the beginning of "modern art." In the Salon of 1787, David exhibited *Death of Socrates*. The painting was immediately hailed as a masterpiece and was compared to Michelangelo's Sistine Chapel ceiling.

By 1789, David became a staunch supporter of the French Revolution. He was a friend and supporter of Robespierre, who would lead the reign of terror a few years later. David was attracted to the high ideals of the republic and embraced the notion of liberty and freedom for all people. In this spirit, he was one of the instigators in attempting to reform the Royal Academy of Painting and Sculpture. He also organized festivals for martyrs who died fighting the royalists. In 1792, David voted along with other members of the National Assembly for the death of the king. This caused his wife, Marguerite-Charlotte, who was a royalist, to divorce him.

David's most famous works of this period right after the revolution were two portraits of the martyrs Le Peletier and Marat. *Le Peletier Assassinated* depicts a bloody sword hanging from a thread, thrust through a note that states "I vote the death of the tyrant." Le Peletier's body is below the sword. Though the original painting has disappeared, drawings and an engraving remain. The other painting, *The Death of Marat*, depicts David's friend Marat dead in a bathtub, writing materials in hand. After the death of the king, the new republic under the leadership of Robespierre attempted to purge itself of all dissenters. The result was the Reign of Terror, during which thousands of French citizens were murdered in the name of the state. In August 1795, when Robespierre was finally seized by the opposition at the National

Convention, David was fortunate to have fallen ill and did not return for the evening session. If he had, he would have been guillotined with Robespierre. Fortunately, his friends intervened and he was jailed for the year.

While in jail, David began to conceive of a painting that depicted the story of the Sabine women. *The Intervention of the Sabine Women* is believed to be in honor of his wife, with its theme of love prevailing over conflict. In 1796, when he was released from prison, he retreated from politics to his studio to work. He took on students again, and his position as premier artist was restored.

Napoleon visited David's studio in 1797 and sat for a portrait. David did not get to finish the portrait because Napoleon left for his Egyptian campaign. David did become Napoleon's favorite painter after his *Napoleon Crossing the Alps* was exhibited. A year later, Napoleon proclaimed David the official court painter of the newly formed French Empire. One of the first works commissioned for the government was *The Coronation of Napoleon in Notre Dame*. In order to paint this work, David attended the coronation. Afterward, he had participants—even the Pope—come to his studio to pose for it. In response to the work, Napoleon said. "David, I salute you."

David's ascension ended with Napoleon's defeat and the return of the Bourbons to the throne. At age 65, David was exiled to Belgium because he had voted to kill the king. There, he painted and lived out the last days of his life quietly with his wife, whom he had remarried. His last great work, *Mars Disarmed by Venus and the Three Graces* was finished the year before his death. He said, "This last picture I want to paint, but I want to surpass myself in it. I will put the date of my seventy-five years on it, and afterward I will never again pick up my brush." The painting was exhibited in Brussels and then in Paris, where more than ten thousand people came to view the masterpiece.

On December 29, 1824, as he was leaving a theater, David was hit by a carriage and died shortly after from deformations of the heart. His body was not allowed to be returned to France and was buried in Brussels, but his heart was buried in Pere Lachaise, Paris.

A Time Line of
Jacques-Louis David's Life

1748   August 30. Jacques-Louis David was born in Paris.

1764   David joins the studio of the artist Vien.

1769   August 15. Napoleon Bonaparte born in Ajaccio, Corsica.

1770   David qualifies in the preliminaries for the painting competition of the Académie Royale de Peinture et de Sculture (the Academy), but does not win a prize.

1771   March 23. Accepted in the final rounds of the Academy's painting competition.

August 31. Receives second prize in painting competition with his entry, *The Combat of Mars and Minerva*.

1772   March 29. Fails in the Academy competition and considers committing suicide.

1773   Awarded the Academy prize for his study of heads and expression.

1774   Louis XV, king of France, dies. Louis XVI ascends the throne.

David receives Academy's first prize in painting for *Antiochus and Stratonice*.

1775–80   Studies painting at the French Academy in Rome.

1780   Exhibits *Saint Roch* in Rome.

1781   David receives a conditional admission to the Royal Academy. He has his first exhibit at the Salon.

1782   David marries Marguerite-Charlotte Pécoul.

1783   Birth of son Jules.

Becomes a full member of the Royal Academy.

Grief of Andromache is exhibited at the Salon.

1784   Birth of son Eugene.

Moves to Rome for the year.

1785   Finishes *The Oath of the Horatii* and exhibits the painting at the Salon. Receives enormous praise.

1786   Birth of twin daughters, Émilie and Pauline.

1787   Exhibits *The Death of Socrates* at the Salon to great acclaim.

1789   July 14. The people revolt in Paris and take the Bastille. The National Assembly is formed and France becomes a constitutional monarchy, with Louis XVI as king.

September. David's *The Lictors Returning to Brutus the Bodies of His Sons* is exhibited at the Salon.

1791   David's first drawing about the events of the revolution, *The Oath of the Tennis Court*, is exhibited at the Salon.

1792   France begins war with Prussia and Austria.

August 10. The French monarchy is overthrown in a popular uprising.

September. France becomes a republic.

September. David is elected deputy from Paris to the National Convention, the country's governing body.

1793   January. David participates with the other deputies of the Convention in condemning Louis XVI to death for treason.

David paints two portraits commemorating martyrs of the revolution: *Le Peletier de Saint-Fargeau* (now lost) and *The Death of Marat*. He donates them to the Convention.

1793–94   The Committee for Public Safety, under the leadership of Robespierre, forms and institutes repression, later called "The Terror."

David organizes revolutionary arts festivals in Paris.

1794   July 27. The National Convention outlaws Robespierre and his cohorts. The Terror ends.

August. David is imprisoned until August 1795 for his role in the repression.

1795   September. A new constitution is formed, and the Directory replaces the National Convention.

1798–99   Bonaparte's Egyptian campaign.

1799   David completes *The Intervention of the Sabine Women.*

November 9. Bonaparte overthrows the Directory and forms the Consulate. He is named First Consul.

1801–03   David paints *Bonaparte Crossing the Alps at Saint Bernard.*

1802   A new constitution names Bonaparte Consul for Life.

1804   May. Napoleon is named "Emperor of the French" under a new constitution.

December 18. David appointed First Painter of the Emperor. He is commissioned to paint the coronation ceremonies of Napoleon and Josephine.

1808   *The Coronation of Napoleon and Josephine* is first exhibited in the Louvre, and later at the Salon.

1810   David paints *The Distribution of the Eagles*, which is exhibited at the Salon.

1812   David paints *The Emperor Napoleon in His Study at the Tuileries.*

1814   April. Napoleon abdicates and is exiled to the island of Elba, off the coast of Italy.

October. David exhibits *Leonidas at Themopylae.*

1815   March. Napoleon returns.

June 18. Napoleon is defeated at the Battle of Waterloo by the British.

June 22. Napoleon abdicates for a second time and is exiled to the island of St. Helena, in the South Atlantic.

1816   January. David is thrown out of France for supporting Napoleon and voting to execute King Louis XVI. He settles in Brussels.

1817   David paints *Cupid and Psyche*.

1818   David paints *The Farewell of Telemachus and Eucharis*.

1819   David paints *The Anger of Achilles*.

1821   May 5. Napoleon dies at St. Helena.

1821–22   David finishes a copy of *The Coronation of Napoleon and Josephine*.

1824   David paints *Mars Disarmed by Venus and the Graces*.

1825   December 29. David dies in Brussels.

Author Bio

Laban Carrick Hill is the author of the Art Encounter series title *Casa Azul: An Encounter with Frida Kahlo*, which was a New York Public Library 2006 Best Book for the Teen Age. His book *Harlem Stomp!* was a National Book Award finalist, a Parent's Choice Gold Award winner, and a *School Library Journal* Best Book of 2004, among other accolades. Hill is the author of more than twenty-five books. He lives in Burlington, Vermont.